Caroline Pitcher x

This Anthology

is gifted to the

Lymphoma Association
(Registered Charity no. 1068395)
www.lymphomas.org.uk

by all of the contributing artists.

All stories, images and graphics are freely donated.
The collection, collation and production of this anthology has
also been gifted free of all charge by

Cybermouse Books

An imprint of;
Cybermouse Multimedia Ltd.,
101 Cross Lane,
Sheffield S10 1WN
www.cybermouse-multimedia.com

**All profits (at least £2 per copy) from the sale of this
Anthology at the printed cover price, will be gifted
directly to The Lymphoma Association (Registered Charity
No. 1068395)**

Although lymphoma is a cancer that affects 14,000 people each year,

…it is not that well known.

While it is the most common form of blood cancer, and most prevalent in people over the age of 55, it is also the most frequently diagnosed cancer amongst young people.

There are no known factors around its incidence or triggers.

It doesn't matter what you've done or haven't done.

There are many different forms, which makes diagnosis and treatment even more complex.

Because of this and many other factors, it's a hard disease to understand and cope with.

Between treatments, 'Watch & Wait' is all you can do.

Through this anthology, we hope to raise awareness of this indiscriminate disease.

Copyrights

Text:	© Each Respective Contributing Author
Graphics:	© W. E. Allerton
Cover font:	© Roland Huse (Rainy Wind)
Cover Image:	© Emma J. Graham
Typeset & Layout:	© W. E. Allerton
Font:	Garamond 12pt.

ISBN: 978-0-9548373-1-0

Published in 2014 by Cybermouse Books

An imprint of;
Cybermouse MultiMedia Ltd.,
101 Cross Lane
Sheffield S10 1WN

www.cybermouse-multimedia.com

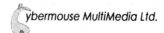

Why this anthology?

You may as well ask, why anything? We wander along through life thinking everything is fine until we run up against something that rocks us back on our heels. If we are very lucky, we never encounter that special something ourselves, but are fated to observe it in others.

For now, it is my fate to be an observer. I'll tell you a story...

One Christmas (my birthday is Christmas Day by the way, which explains a lot about my complex), Bryony, my partner, found it difficult to come up with an original present. As I'd been learning (hah!) the guitar, I thought that singing lessons might be a good idea. I suppose that 'good' is entirely subjective, depending on whether you're singing or listening, but I digress as usual.

Bryony found someone who was prepared to try and teach an irreverent ineducable, such as myself, the rudiments of the vocal arts.

Well... we tried, or rather *he* tried. The sessions ended up in gales of laughter and spent wit but with little in the way of vocal advancement. I will state here that he had the ability to be a fine teacher, after all that's what he used to do as a profession, but I lack the ability to be a fine pupil.

To cut this short, he became 'my mate Andrew', the brother I never had.

Andrew is living with lymphoma, and Bryony and I have spent some time sitting around hospital beds with the rest of his harem of well-wishers while he has undergone chemotherapy, new knees and other essential indignities brought about largely by the progression of this condition.

Throughout all this, Andrew has maintained a stoic sense of humour and good nature, always looking after others before himself while arranging care homes and assistance for those he considered less well equipped to survive than he.

I come away from this with an overwhelming sense of admiration for his courage, and an understanding that an Andrew Is For Life, not Just For Christmas.

To see for yourself what it means to live with lymphoma, please visit the following YouTube video:
http://bit.ly/1iHJEm8

I would like to particularly thank the following for their support in this project;

Andrew Nimmo, for his help in the initial concept.
Each author who has gifted their work.
Julie Brazier, for her help in the proofing of manuscripts.
Emma J. Graham, for her inspired cover image.

I dedicate this anthology to Andrew, and all others living with lymphoma.

Bill Allerton

Cybermouse Multimedia Ltd.

Watch

&

Wait.

Authors

Angela Robson

is an award-winning writer, broadcaster and film-maker.

As a foreign correspondent for the BBC, Le Monde Diplomatique, Aljazeera and The Guardian, she has reported from over fifty countries.

Angela's love of writing and journalism began when she found herself in Sierra Leone during the beginning of the civil war in 1986. Her feature made the front cover and a centre spread of The Independent. This was the trigger she needed to leave her then position with a major human rights organisation and embrace the world of writing and journalism full-time.

Her awards since include the European Commission's Natali Lorenzo Prize (first prize for Europe) for her article, 'Sierra Leone: Revenge and Reconciliation' and the Guardian International Development Journalism Prize for a series of reports about sexual violence in Haiti. Her documentary about deforestation and land-grabs in Ghana was runner-up winner for the British Media and Environment Award.

Angela holds a Master's degree in English from the University of Toronto, Canada, and a BA Hons. in English Literature from the University of York.

She is currently working on her first novel, Aftershocks, set in Haiti.

The Jungle Palace

The pathway leading to the house is knotted with vines. Jungle has reclaimed the pink concrete car park and the elaborately laid-out gardens. The door is open.

The building is filled with light.

Guests would not have known where to look first on entering – the huge fake stalactites, the imposing oak panelled bar area, the ceiling-high windows gaping outwards, or the pool with its mosaic of the Liberian flag emblazoned on the red and white striped tiles.

A waiter would have provided the answer, gesturing them to come to the bar, offering them beers. The President is on his way down.

Samuel Doe's unfinished dream house, this three-story mansion here in Zwedru, forest capital of Liberia's Grand Gedeh county, was scheduled for completion in the summer of '91. The underground escape tunnel had been finished first.

What were his thoughts, I wonder, when they captured him in Monrovia? The first interrogation lasts fourteen minutes, filmed throughout on a shaky video camera - a film that will later make the rounds of most cinemas in Liberia.

You can watch the soldiers trying to tug off his shirt, incapable of wrestling it over his shackled hands. They smash his thick glasses, then remove the green army trousers.

His large white underpants are smeared with bloody streaks.

Beneath a picture of Christ, his rival Prince Johnson swills cans of Heineken and asks Doe for his bank account numbers.

I recall the last image of him:

Legs, strong and muscular, arms and chest powerful. Disfigured head hidden, his body dwarfs the triumphant rag-tag of adolescent boys brandishing Kalashnikovs and wild stares that surround him, their bandanas inlaid with shiny brass bullets.

I think of Doe's wife, wondering if she ever saw this. She will know the details, how they first cut off his ear with a dirty penknife while two men pinned him to the ground.

This house fit for a president was abandoned by builders the following day. The windows are open to the elements now. Pools of brown water have collected on the cream marble staircases and the mahogany floors.

Swallows flit in and out, regardless of my presence, nesting in the creepers growing up the grey, cracked walls.

Wedding Pictures

I had heard that you were unusually tall, even for a white woman. Hair brown and curly; beautiful and fearless. I can deal with beauty. It is the fearlessness that makes me wary.

I watch you approach the front gate, a little too confidently for a first visit. Did you think, because you are young, that I would treat you delicately? Did you presume that we would become best friends?

You smile when I open the door. 'I was just passing. I saw the house name, the number. I didn't expect...'

'You didn't expect what?' I reply, trying to be polite.

'I wanted to see...' you continue. 'Well, you know, I felt it was right to greet you. I didn't expect you to be in.'

Why come then? I want to say. *Why captivate my husband in Nairobi with your slender ankles, your concern for the child soldiers of Africa?*

'We are *all* in,' I answer firmly, trying to keep the anger out of my voice.

You enter without invitation, up the stairs and straight into the second living room. I can tell that you are surprised by the house – the cream leather sofas, the silver table in the centre of the room, the white grand piano.

Am I the person you presumed I would be? Someone who will be reserved and deferential? Who will say nothing about the double-page spread in the newspaper? The vivid account of your life in the African bush as the wife of a rebel leader? The photo in front of your small mud hut, wearing your long floating skirt and African beads with your arms around his neck?

You turn away from the window, 'It's a shame about the traffic noise.'

'There is no traffic noise,' I reply. 'And besides, we like living on a busy road.'

'But why Swiss Cottage?'

'Why not? It is near the children's schools. It is close to the embassies. It is good for diplomats.'

'Malek is not a diplomat.'

'But I am.'

You look shocked, though you try not to let me notice it. He will not have told you that part of the story.

Does my husband see you in the same way I do? Is he too dark to notice the large black irises in your grey-green eyes, the pale freckles on the small upturned nose? Does he not see what I see?

'I didn't know they dressed boys like that.' The words tumble out of your mouth before you can help it.

My youngest son has crept in quietly and wrapped himself around my right calf.

'It is traditional cloth,' I reply. 'You haven't come across this in our country?'

But you are not listening. On your face there is a stung expression. Your man in my child's face. Large, inquiring eyes. Blue-black shining skin. The boy Malek is most protective of. Where you think I am not an obstacle, my child is.

It is clear you want to know everything, thirsty for details so that you can construct the jigsaw of Malek's life before your arrival. You do not want straightforward answers. No, you are too complex for that. You need the blow to the stomach encounters such as ours will deliver.

'He wants a feed,' I say, sensing what this will trigger.

'You're breastfeeding, still?'

'He's only thirteen months, he still wants it.'

If it is too much for you, this reminder that my child's conception was not so long ago, I will tell you, also, that my skin will age differently from yours; my belly will never show the stretch marks of pregnancy.

We have heard it so often. The white girl who comes to the dark continent, who feels alive for the first time. Our men are excited when you wear our glinting beads around your waist and head down to the beach after sunset.

You understand polygamy, you told the newspaper reporter. It is an African tradition which is never going to change. Far better for it to be sanctioned and accepted.

I pick up the boy and give him my breast.

Berlie Doherty

has written over 60 books as well as plays for radio, theatre and television, short stories and poetry. She has won major awards and prizes in all fields, including the Carnegie Medal (twice), the Writers' Guild award (twice), Film and Television Award and Royal Philharmonic Society award (for a libretto), and was shortlisted for the International Astrid Lingren award.

Berlie has been published in 21 different languages, and has travelled the world extensively, speaking at International literature festivals and conferences.

She began over 30 years ago by writing short stories for BBC Radio 4 Morning Story, and has published one short story collection, 'Running on Ice'. Much of her writing is for young adults, though she also writes picture book texts, children's books and has two novels for adults, 'Requiem' and 'The Vinegar Jar', both of which are due to be republished in 2014 by Cybermouse MultiMedia Ltd.

Berlie is best known for 'Dear Nobody', which won many awards both as a young adult novel and as a play for theatre and for radio. It has also been made into a television drama.

Her book for children, 'Street Child', (also a play script) is read and performed extensively in schools throughout the country, and she is currently completing a long-awaited sequel.

'Crossing the Glacier' won First prize in the Daily Telegraph short story competition and was published in the Daily Telegraph Book of Contemporary Short Stories. It has also been broadcast on BBC Radio 4.

You can follow Berlie at www.berliedoherty.com or on Twitter, where she reveals the life of a writer.

Her most recent novel is 'The Company of Ghosts'.

Crossing the Glacier

It was three years since Gerda's husband had died. The memory of his going was always there, like ice around her heart.

She had a lovely house in the mountains. They'd worked hard for it. Her daughter Inga spent her holidays there these days, bringing the grandsons with her. This time she tried to persuade Gerda to sell the house and move south so they could be closer together.

The two women took the boys up into the forest to forage for bilberries and wild raspberries.

'Come home with us,' Inga urged her mother.

'I love it here.' Gerda did not expect her daughter to understand. 'I can't go back to the city now.'

'What is it that keeps you here? It can't be the campsite.'

'In a way, it is,' Gerda said. She didn't expect Inga to understand that, either.

'It's so tying for you. Such long hours, such a short season in this country. It's hardly worth it.'

'It pays for my holidays,' Gerda said, a little dreamily. 'The campsite has always been my job.'

When Stefan was alive she had been proud to pay with her own earnings for the October coach trips they took to Austria and Switzerland or the French Alps, visiting the mountains of other countries.

Stefan had given her the mountains long ago, when she was scarcely more than a child. Now she was uncomfortable away from them, or from the sound of the rushing milky blue beck that ran outside her house. She loved the campers to come and share it with her. They were like her family. They liked her site because of the beck, but it was too swift for their canoes, and too deathly cold to swim in. She laughed to see their faces when they tried. Why, the glacier it came from was little more than two kilometres away! You had only to glance up to see it there, a crinkled curtain of ice hanging over the valley.

She stood up, stretching her back. Above the trees the white tips of the mountains glimmered.

'And it keeps me busy.'

Gerda would sit every day from nine in the morning till nine at night, June to September, in the log cabin between the campers' toilets and the showers. She had her television in there, turned down low, and she always listened out for the weather forecast so she could pass it on to her campers. She loved to be able to tell them there was good weather to come. There was so much rain here.

'I suppose it stops you from being lonely,' Inga said later, just before she left. She was standing with her back to the house where she had been born. In the campsite at the bottom of the lane she could hear children playing. 'That's a good thing.'

It was true that there were always campers to talk to. People tended not to stay very long though. They'd book in for a couple of days, do the guided glacier walk, and then be off to the fjords and into the serious walking country of the Jutenheimen.

So the English woman fascinated Gerda. She came on her own, which was quite unusual for a female camper, and she didn't seem to want to leave. She stayed for days and days, just booking in a night at a time. Her car, with its GB sticker and the black stripes stuck across the headlamps, hardly ever moved from the site. She strolled up to the mountain every day, or along the beck, read a lot, and when Gerda closed up her cabin she was always bedded down for the night, her tent zipped up, no light on. Gerda watched her and worried about her. That woman is unhappy, she thought.

One evening she waited until the English woman had finished her meal and was carrying her bowl of dishes back from the washing-up cabin to her tent. Instead of scurrying in after her to check whether the floor needed mopping, Gerda followed her down the field, calling out a greeting.

'You seem to like being here.'

She joined the woman by the beck, where the pale apple-mint water creamed over the white slabs of the boulders.

'Oh, I do. It's a beautiful place. The facilities are very clean.'

'Thank you,' Gerda murmured. 'And tomorrow the weather will be fine. We should not have had today's rain. It has come up from Oslo, but the TV did not foretell of it.'

'Forecast it. Good, I'm glad it will be fine.' The woman hesitated, her bowl of dishes in her arms.

'You have come here to walk in the mountains?'

'Sort of.' She half-laughed, put down her bowl and stood slightly turned away from Gerda, her hand shielding her eyes.

'I came to walk on that thing, actually.'

'The glacier. Of course. Everybody does.' Gerda was proud. 'It is an extraordinary phenomenon, is it not? Eternal ice.'

'Quite a terrifying thing to have hanging over your house.' The woman laughed. 'You've been across it, of course?'

'Only once,' Gerda said, after a pause. 'I walked once on that glacier.' And walked away from my childhood, she thought. 'A long time ago.'

The English woman laughed ruefully. 'I came here to do it, and I must do it, but I can't. It's so stupid. I go up to where the walk starts and I see people being roped up by the guide, and I can't make myself do it.'

'Why must you?' asked Gerda. 'Perhaps it is enough to come here and admire it.'

It began to rain, and both women turned away. Gerda went back to her cabin and flicked through the selection of postcards that she kept in stock for the campers. They were of the glacier in all its different moods, and they were all, she thought, ugly. They showed a grey crinkled skin, like the hide of an elephant. That was not how she remembered it. 'You have to look into the heart of it.' She could remember Stefan saying that to her as if it had been yesterday.

When she went home that night she paused for a moment outside the hut where her husband's climbing equipment was kept - boots, ropes, ice axes, crampons. She had not looked at them since his death. She had not been able to.

The next day was as beautiful as her TV had promised it would be, a perfect crisp Norwegian day with the sky empty of clouds and the beck sparkling back the sunshine. Gerda beamed at her campers as she passed them, delighted for them. The English woman came to book in for another night, and Gerda gave her the best of the postcards.

'I'll send it to my son,' the woman said. 'He does stuff like this - glacier walking, mountaineering, skiing, all that kind of thing.' She put the card quickly into her bag and raised her hands in a little, hopeless gesture. 'That's why I came really. I just want to know what it's like, that's all. His world.'

'You should have brought him with you. Or is he too old now for holidays with his mother?'

'We used to do everything together. I never even lived with his father. It's always been just me and Sandy. And now he's gone to University and he's started a new life that I don't know anything about. I can't talk to him about anything any more. Abseiling, that's another thing he does. I thought it was something to do with yachts!'

A child came running to Gerda to say there was a rat in his tent. Gerda picked up a brush and ran after the boy, apologising as she went. A few minutes later a small brown and tan creature darted down to the beck, chased by Gerda.

'I want you to know,' Gerda said, panting, 'that it was not a rat in the tent. I do not have rats. I have lemmings. All it can do is scream, silly creature. Sometimes they scream themselves to death, but no harm done.'

'It's all right,' the English woman smiled. 'They're all over the mountain, those things. I thought they were guinea pigs actually.'

'You go and walk that glacier!' Gerda said to her. 'You've come all this way, and you've experienced rain and lemmings. Do what you came for!'

She found herself watching out all day for the English-woman's return. When she saw her at last she called out eagerly. 'Yes?'

The woman shook her head. She came over to the cabin.

'I'm hopeless, aren't I? Hopeless! All I want to do is to go home and say to Sandy, 'Guess what I did in Norway!' She laughed. 'And I can't do it.'

Why do people hide their pain in laughter, Gerda wondered.

'You are afraid to do it,' she said. 'There's no shame in that. You're afraid of falling?'

'Not falling. Failing. That guide up there is only a kid. He's younger than Sandy. What will he do if I stand in the middle of his roped line and… cry? Can't go forwards or backwards? Just cry? What could he do to help me?'

'Now I understand,' said Gerda. 'Now I understand everything.'

When they had brought her news of her husband's death she had not cried. They were strangers who had found his half-frozen body on the mountain. What was her grief to do with them? She had stood and watched the silent roped procession bringing him home to her. Like tidy shopkeepers, the strangers had arranged his climbing things in her hut. She had thanked them, but she had not cried.

'Today,' Gerda said, 'you will walk across the glacier.'

She recognised the start of panic in the woman's face. She had felt like that when the same words had been spoken to her forty years before.

'Today? But won't it be too late? The walk finishes at six.'

'I will go with you.'

Gerda took her to her own house, through the living room with the lovely carved and gilded cupboards that Stefan had made. She opened the door to the hut. It smelt of Stefan. It was a good smell of leather and wax and metal. From the collection of crampons that had been her daughter's they chose pairs that fitted their own walking boots. Then Gerda picked out ice axes, harnesses, and a rope. 'We will take food and hot drinks,' she said. 'It will take a long time, and it will be hard work.'

When they were ready she held out her hand in a cordial, shy way. 'I am asking you to trust me with your life,' she said. 'And all I know about you is the registration number of your car.'

'I'm Pam,' the English woman said.

'And I am Gerda.'

When they arrived at the snout of the glacier the mountain was deserted except for a large grey-brown bird flapping around the white boulders. The pool below the glacier was a deep, still blue. Above the women the crinkled ice-cliffs sheered up, a huge stretch of silence into the sky. The women scrambled over the smooth boulders, hot with effort, exhausting themselves with their haste. As soon as they came to the hem of the ice skirt, Pam lost her footing. She clung on to Gerda.

'I can't,' she said. 'We'll kill ourselves.'

'It is important for you to know how treacherous the ice is,' Gerda said, remembering her husband's words. 'You are not in control. Now try your crampons, and you will trust them.'

They fastened the spiked crampon shields around their boots. Gerda showed Pam how to place her feet firm and flat as she walked, how to walk sideways up and down slopes. She showed her how to use the spiked end of her ice axe like a walking stick, and how to grip the ice sideways with the blade. Then she fastened their harnesses and tied the rope that held them together, like an umbilical cord, and showed her how it must hang, not trailing, not tight, between them.

'Now.' Gerda turned away from Pam and stared up at the cliffs of the glacier. 'We are ready.'

The two women stepped cautiously onto the ice and, little by little, began to haul themselves up the sides of the first corridor. Gerda was no more confident than Pam. She felt as if she was leading her own child unwillingly into darkness. And curiously, she felt herself to be that child, to have become again a young girl who had never left her parents' side, making that journey again for the first time, for Stefan's sake. She scrambled up onto the first ledge and waited for Pam to join her.

The ice was as beautiful to her now as it was all those years ago. She had forgotten. She peered down into the whorls and crevasses, into the intense blue of its steep gulleys, into the deep ravines of the mountain beneath her feet. Spindrift wind had crested the surface like lacy coral.

As the rope slackened and she heard Pam's gasping breath behind her she stamped again into the surface, finding purchase with the spikes of her crampons, anchoring herself against the sheer slip of ice beneath her feet. Her face was taut and set, intent on her task. Her breath came in long labouring gasps, wrenched from such depths that she could have thought it was from the mountain itself.

Then she heard a thin, reedy spiral of sound that seemed to rise from the ice. She stopped, marvelling at its fragile loveliness, and realised that the sound was human. She turned round to see that Pam was singing.

'Happy?' Gerda laughed.

'More than I've ever been in my life! I can't believe I'm doing this!'

'We should have a photograph to show your son!'

'I didn't bring my camera,' said Pam. 'I didn't really think we'd do it!' Unexpectedly and without control she started laughing.

Gerda felt a sudden gush of movement inside her head. She turned away. Something was welling up in her that could not be controlled or quenched, rearing like a wild thing out of her heart. She cupped both her hands to her mouth but the thing was not to be held back. Her limbs heaved with the power of it. She sank to her knees and cried for Stefan, as she had never been able to cry before.

Pam, shocked, edged across the ice towards her. She looked down at Gerda and then knelt next to her, holding out her hands, just touching the older woman's shoulders. She cried with her. At last the terrible sound of grief quietened down to whimpers, and then into silence.

'There comes a time,' Pam said aloud, not even realising she was saying it, 'When you have to let go. I understand that now.'

Next day Pam packed up her tent while the dew was still on the grass. Gerda waved her goodbye and went to her cabin. She switched on the TV to catch the first weather forecast and did her round of cleaning the toilets and showers. Everything was spotless. She would leave it that way. She would close the site early this year. She would have a holiday by the sea for a change, with the grandchildren. She would arrange it this morning.

She glanced up at the glacier hanging half in mist, half in sunlight, like a huge curtain across the end of the valley.

'I know you now,' she said. 'And I am free.'

Bill Allerton

lives, sleeps, drinks, writes and worries in his native city of Sheffield - where he currently has too much work in progress.

His involvements have included:

The collation and production of a photographic, musical and poetic journey through the Five Weirs Walk in Sheffield.

The creation of Networx, a literary organisation that drew together writers groups from across the Yorkshire region. As a result of their involvement, a member group went on to create the Rotherham Literature Festival.

A short story in the winning Fish Prize Anthology and subsequent reading at the West Cork Literature Festival.

Various pieces for online science-fiction magazines, 'Beyond the Brink' and 'Cluster'.

The performance of eight stories for BBC local radio.

The adaptation of his prize-winning short story, 'To Kill a Wish' at The Pomegranate Theatre, Chesterfield, as part of the New Playwrights season.

The production of a book of short stories and narrative poems created with the children of Sharrow School in Sheffield. 'Y2 Stories'

Bill's first novel, 'The Fox & The Fish' continues to receive extremely favourable reviews.

Bill is now MD of Cybermouse Multimedia Ltd.

Red Stripe Candy

'Libby!'

Virna Morrell occupies the corner by the slatted french window like a jewelled ornament shrouded in black lace. When she speaks, only her lips move, only her breath scatters motes in the bracketed light.

'Comin' Miss Virna.'

Libby's voice carries in from the kitchen on a wave of cooking smells. There is cabbage, and all kinds of green stuff cut fresh from a garden now hemmed by weeds and brought closer to the house by each season.

'Hey, Libby!'

'Yes, Miss Virna.'

'Libby! It's almost two o'clock.'

'Comin', Miss Virna.'

The clock in the hall starts its groan as Libby pulls herself through from the kitchen. In the drawing room, each piece of furniture waits to fall under her familiar hand.

'Better than kin,' she would always say, 'At least you knows where it stands!'

Libby brakes the wheels on Miss Virna's chair with a foot she can hardly see for the swelling in her ankles. She straightens the bright-flowered print of her frock with one hand and with the other she pushes back a stray lock of hair and wipes the pain from her face.

'Now then, Miss Virna. What you wanna see today?'

'The train, Libby. The train.'

'Just th' old milk run, Miss Virna, T'aint nuthin' special.'

Virna remains silent, her eyes fixed on the slats of the right hand shutter where it hangs, waiting for the years in Libby's gnarled and broken hands to shake the rust from the hinges.

'If I opens th'other side, p'raps we'll see the Reverend and his pretty wife in their new car. You knows they always wave an'... the way her face lits up a dull day! Like your sister you say, back in '34. But Abby would've been 'bout thirty then and this one cain't be no more than, oh, twenty three or so, and her with them two kids runnin' round like peas in a pod...'

Virna's gaze remains fixed on the right hand shutter. If she sits perfectly still, like a dark butterfly resting... all folded wings and withdrawn, inwardly-directed senses... then at two o'clock each day between mid-May and August... on days when the sky is open and wide, not closed and shuttered and dark with clouds like this room in which she sits... the sun will chip sparks from the gold on her fingers and shimmer the inlaid silver and mother-of-pearl around her throat. Her head will lean forwards and a little to one side, and she will smile her only smile in the shadow of Libby's relentless chatter.

'...an' when the clock strikes we can watch it shower the old-town with doves, an' some o' them dirty grey pigeons they seem to 've taken up with. Cain't say I like grey. Was grey the day I buried my daddy. Was grey the day I got the letter sayin' my Joseph weren't never comin' back an' it's grey when I look in the mirror. And the pain! Some people say pain's red. But I tell you it ain't so. Pain's grey!'

'The train, Libby.'

'Yes Ma'am, Miss Virna.'

'Can't help but see the church whichever way I look, Libby.'

'Yes Ma'am, Miss Virna. The train it is. Choo Choo.'

'Shut up, Libby.'

'Yes Ma'am... Miss Virna.'

Outside the french windows the air falls still, like the world holding its breath and waiting for summer to steal in unannounced, the ground barely dry from last nights shower. Beyond a quarter acre of grass stands a row of tall cypress trees, their flame shapes casting fine, filigreed shadows over the lawn.

Hemmings planted the trees in his thirtieth year so that Miss Virna didn't have to see the way that the houses and sheds and streets and the bus station had crept steadily up towards the old house. As the town grew, the trees stretched up and wide as if conspiring to keep the worst of the days from her. Now, they filter the street noises from the air, and when the wind blows they bend with an old-fashioned grace to protect the shingle roof.

Seen from beyond the hedge the house is enigmatic, something of an anachronism. It looms like an elder sister over the small, white, clapboard church at the bottom of the drive as though they are locked... religion just a curve away from tradition... a slow crunch of gravel apart.

Virna understands that journey almost as well as she understands herself. It feels like yesterday, but it's a journey she hasn't made in twenty-five years.

To the right of the church, over by a street of low black-pitch-roof garages and kiosks, stands the Station. Its gable roof is canted so high above the tracks that on hot days the sun slides under and around it so that it's mostly no use at all. The broad white gingerbread fascias were once lovingly re-painted every two years by Jackson, the retired engine driver come Station Master, porter, painter... well, almost anything that needed doing... but now his broken ladder frames the flowers that grow in a twenty-foot bed behind the platform.

From the office window Jackson can see the old house, and although from his chair he can't see her... not like forty years or so ago, when he could've counted the birds in the hedgerow and admired the slim, brown stretch of Miss Libby's legs as she tidied the garden... he can still imagine that Miss Virna, punctual as ever, is sitting behind one shutter and peering out through the other where it swings wide on the world.

He had once asked her why she didn't just throw them both open and have done.

'Too much world at once, Mr Jackson.' she had said, 'I don't think I was made for that much world at once.'

She never had called him to the house again, and sometimes it felt as though he'd just sat back to watch the dust settle on and around her.

From the side of a rail baking in the early summer heat, a flake of rust falls into the gravel bed. The iron sings softly to itself and the station cat opens one slow, haunted eye.

Jackson takes a last look up the hill towards Miss Virna in her chair, in her prison, in her own time. Around him, the Station waits, open mouthed, dust settling quietly on its fifteen-year paintwork.

'Say, Libby?'
'Yes'm?'

'I was just 'minded of red-stripe candy.'

'Now there's a thing.'

Virna scowls at the implied sarcasm, 'The train's late.'

'No, Ma'am. Clock's fast. Church ain't struck yet.'

Virna listens lightly for the urgent throb of the diesel engine entering the ravine, her thoughts running barefoot, 'Red-stripe candy.'

'Yes'm?'

'The preacher's boys. I swear they smelled of red-stripe candy. You remember, the kind that's all spirals of white and red and peppermint taste and bent at the end like a walking stick? I could smell it for hours after they'd gone.'

She sniffs the air sharply.

'There! Still a trace. Just a trace though, it's fading now. Can't you smell it Libby?'

'No Ma'am. I sure cain't. Them boys haven't been here in years.'

'Libby! They were here just the other day.'

'No Ma'am. Sure as I'm here.'

'You're getting old, Libby.'

'Sure am, Miss Virna. From haulin' you around in that damn chair.'

Though familiar, Libby's remark passes across Virna's thoughts like a dark hand. She has felt old for almost as long as she can remember, except for that one time... and that one time had made the scar that left her in this chair and waiting for a darker comfort.

'Libby!'

'Yes, Miss Virna?'

'My best shawl.'

'Company comin'?'

'Don't know, Libby. I just know I need my best shawl.'

Libby negotiates the furniture to the hallway. From there, she sits at the bottom of the stairs and shuffles her way up, one step at a time.

From behind the closed left shutter Virna's eyes pierce the distance until they blur upon the open mouth of the Station. The church clock hangs at a few minutes to two. The chimes of the hall clock are five long minutes gone, pushed by silence into the all too easily forgotten past.

Libby pauses at the top of the stairs to catch her breath and allow the pounding in her body to subside. Through the silence of the house, she listens to the drum of occluded arteries in her head.

Hemmings is outside tidying the kitchen garden, stoking the mulch back around the cabbages where Libby used to stump between the rows, looking for the best of the early ones. The afternoon sun is warm on his back, easing tomorrow's pain from his muscles. As he works his way along the side of the house to where the garden is edged by lawn, he stops to light his pipe.

Earlier this morning the wind had sighed gently through the cypress trees, trimming their leaves towards the house, trapping within themselves the sounds of cars and children and the clang and shut of businesses that are kept at bay by the sheer presence of the old house, but now there is silence. The air is still, as if the world and it's neighbour are on vacation and he alone is left with a chance to relax and edge the lawn in peace without the sounds of dogs barking... or the smell of barbecued grease clinging to his summer shirt.

Enjoying the moment, Hemmings sits by the edge of the lawn, pipe warm in his cupped hand, the uneven charcoal rim dark against the slow fire of his memories.

Upstairs, Libby lifts Miss Virna's best shawl to her face and breathes in through the black Parisienne lace. It holds a faint but pervasive scent of peppermint. It lingers in her mind as she stretches the cloth over her fingers to rub at the coarseness of its weave with her thumb, feeling the patterns under her skin and experiencing the darkness within the folds.

Going down the stairs will be easier with lungs that don't ache and a chest that doesn't pound and a head that is more silent than hers right now, so she sits on the edge of the bed for a while, enveloped in the peppermint scent from the shawl.

The church clock strikes a knell into the warmth of the mid-afternoon. Doves rocket out from the belfry louvres and settle with the grace of confetti on the surrounding outhouse roofs. Miss Virna watches them dispassionately from a corner of her eye while she times the coming of the second knell with precision. The clapboard sides and the quarter-paned windows of the house take the sound with an easy grace.

'It's late, Libby.'

Libby is taking the stairs one step at a time, the shawl thrown across her own shoulders and shaming the crystal grey in her hair.

Virna's eyes never waver from the gaping mouth of the Station roof.

'Libby! Libby! Where is that girl?'

Libby stumps from the hat rack to the calling-card table by the hall door.

'Pray tell where should I be, Miss Virna?'

'Right here. By me. Where you belong.'

Libby drapes the shawl across Miss Virna's shoulders, adjusting the length against the chair back.

'I swear some days I don't know who belongs where or to what 'cept I wouldn't care if only these legs belonged somebody else that's all 'cept I cain't think of anybody I hates that much 'cept...'

'Shut up, Libby.'

'Yes Ma'am, Miss Virna.'

'The train's late, Libby.'

'Yes Ma'am, Miss Virna.'

The room shakes to the gentle thunder of a train travelling the ravine that separates the house from the suburban sprawl to the east. Miss Virna nods satisfactorily as if the coming of the train has turned a chapter in her book, or maybe marked the ever-shortening calendar in her head.

Out by the mulch bin, Hemmings coughs in a sudden pall of dark smoke that billows up from the divide. He hears the throttle eased as the train sleee-s to a halt in the Station.

Jackson jumps up with a bound he had lately thought beyond all expectation. The cat cowers beneath a trolley, away from the shooting, reaching, twisting steam and the hiss and sudden heat of hot black iron. Jackson closes his eyes to sniff the air. It's a steamer alright, a 4-6-2 Pacific on a high-slung frame with super-heat and double acting cylinders, just like the one that finished his days and still screams its way through his dreams of a night, but what the hell is it doing here in all its black-spit an' brass-polish glory?

The engine is magnificent, so far beyond human scale and yet monstrously alive. The driving wheels are wider than Jackson could span with both arms and in the places where they have met the steel rails they are polished with the sheen of a thousand, thousand miles. The footplate is empty. He steps up.

His lungs fill with the scent of tar bubbling from the seams in the swelling coals where they stir, bursting fire and flame under the boiler. He climbs back down to the platform where the taste of hot grease oozing from the axle boxes and brake trunnions is a tangible thing. He takes a breath of steam, and feels it invades his tissue like the first faint tang of peppermint.

Behind the night-black of the engine the silent carriages shimmer mid-brown in the sunlight. A gold inlay runs at waist height on a line through the handles. On tiptoe, Jackson peers through the first window. It is dark inside and at first seems empty, but as he looks he thinks to see movement, then dismisses it as steam wisps the glass.

Along the platform he hears the snick of a brass coach-handle. A door swings wide to show rich leather upholstery. A man steps down beside the track. He speaks quietly, and with the ease of familiarity.

'Hello, Roy.'

Libby takes the chair by Miss Virna and curves her spine against the high back. Virna sits watching the Station mouth spill and overflow with cotton-candy clouds.

'Say, Libby? Is the Station afire?'

'Cain't say for sure, Miss Virna. I b'lieve it might be.'

'Look! There's Jackson comin' up the hill. Who's the young man with him?'

'Cain't say, Miss Virna, your eyes better'n mine. You been savin' yours an' usin' mine for years.'

'Now, Libby!'

'Yes Ma'am, Miss Virna.'

Roy Jackson takes the first fifty feet of the hill with a deceptive ease, but he stops there to shake the hand of a smartly dressed young man and to wave him on up to the old house. The man takes the next fifty yards before he begins to slow. Roy notices the left leg take on a cautious swing that turns gradually into a well-defined limp as he walks on. Twitching forward as the man stumbles, Roy relaxes again as he rights himself and carries on up the hill, a little more stooped now than before. Past the halfway mark, the man pauses to push something into the hedgerow that hems the drive.

Unable to see what it was, Roy turns around and walks back to the Station.

'Libby! He's comin' here.'

'Nah. He's probl'y callin' to the church. Looks like a preacher in that there high collar.'

'No. Look. He's already passed the church. But the hill's takin' its toll... such a shame... he set off so well an' all...'

'Strikes me a little unsteady on his feet, Miss Virna. Prob'ly a liquor salesman.'

'You know Jackson wouldn't send a liquor salesman up here.'

Libby leans forward to rub at the corner of a glass pane.

'Well, he's comin' here whoever he is. Looks kinda old though to be comin' up the hill in this heat.'

Between intakes of breath, Virna hears the slow, unsteady crunch of gravel as the man passes around the front of the house to the porch at the rear. The doorbell rings.

'Libby! Get the door. Hurry, girl.'

The furniture waits patiently as Libby patterns her way back into the hall. Virna hears the door being swung wide and a warm swath of minted summer air finds her where she sits behind the half shutter.

Libby returns carrying a small silver salver from the card-table in the hall. In her other hand is a gnarled walking stick that begins where the brown swirl of her fingers leaves off.

'Cain't say I remember folks still did this. Cain't say it ain't nothin' but a joke anyway!'

'What is it Libby? Bring it here to the light.'

Libby is visibly trembling.

26

'Cain't say you should trouble yourself...'

She drops the stick on the floor with a jarring clatter.

'Bring it here, girl.'

'No Ma'am, Miss Virna.'

'Bring it!'

'Yes Ma'am, Miss Virna.'

Virna plucks the card from the tray and turns it over onto her own hand. It drops into her lap as if it was iced and the merest touch of her skin had melted and slid it out of her grasp.

'Libby! What kind of a joke is this?'

'T'aint none what I'd call funny, Miss Virna.'

Virna studies the card, hoping for some mistake, but there it lay, edged in gold with a kind of wavy trim and small fancy holes punched in around the edges through which an enterprising young girl might thread a ribbon... a ribbon that she had shaken loose from her hair one early summer day... like the one outside...

'Send him away!'

'She can't do that, Virna, I just plain won't go.'

Virna turns her head slowly at the remembered richness of a man's voice, then quickly away again before she can see his face.

'And I say she can!'

Libby is standing behind Miss Virna's chair and staring fixedly out of the window as if she is afraid to look at the old man stooped by the doorway.

'If Miss Virna says I can, then mister, you better.'

'And who's going to pull you out the pond this time Libby? All shakin' wet an' mixin' with tears. An' who's going to lift you down from the orchard after Miss Virna done got you stuck up there again, chasing for moon-sized apples?'

Libby is shaking like she was still stood on that high wall, the tremor of her hands fluttering the black of the shawl as they hold to the chair.

'Don't you say those things. You hear me? Just don't you say 'em!'

Virna turns her face back to the window.

'You should listen to the girl, Richard. There's no cause for you to find us again at this end of our lives. It was better you hadn't come.'

'Do you know what a circle is Virna? It's a twist of rope that's full of beginnings because it has no end and so what else could it be made of?'

Virna sits, stony-faced, 'You broke our circle and you broke me and you broke this blasted hip and you took away my dancing shoes and my candles and music and nights without pain and summer grasses running wild under my feet and just... Go away.'

She closes her eyes, 'I wish you away. If all you can do after seventy years is talk in circles.'

The old man follows Libby's path through the drawing room. He catches her looking and smiles. She turns away from him back to the view outside the window.

'Life's a circle, Virna.'

'Have you looked in my mirror lately, Richard? This is what I look like at the end. An' I sure as hell don't need reminding.'

'This isn't the end, Virna. I'm here to show you how to begin.'

'A fine time, I'm sure. Libby! Get the door. The gentleman is leaving.'

'Nothing has to end, Virna. Look...' he holds a hand out into the air between them, '...there are so many beginnings if we just reach out and take them. They're like orchard apples on a fall day. They're everywhere you look. On the floor, in the air and hung around every which way in-between. You just pick the one that takes your fancy and bite right in! And if that don't work out or the worm beat you to it, you find a better one and try again.'

'And where was my beginning, Richard? Did I begin to dance again? Did I begin with gentlemen by the rack and my tray full of gilt-edged cards? Did I begin to forgive you for spookin' my buggy with that damned automobile?'

'Oh, you began alright, Virna. You began to suck in all that was sour and bitter and lost in the world. You began to close in on yourself and the people around you until we felt we were nothin' compared to your pain. You began to end. You bit that apple, worm an' all and you never threw anything away. It's all still there, stuffed like a cushion beneath you so you can sit there in your own shadow and brood about all the things that ended, just so you don't have to look up and see all these beginnings hanging in the air around you. Oh yes, you began alright.'

'If I ever began, Richard, it ended the day I sent you away.'

'And now I'm here to show you how to start again, Virna.'

'I'm sorry Richard, but my end is close upon me and your fine talk won't stop me or any of us from reaching it, one way or another.'

'Come with me, Virna. You too, Libby.'

'You cain't take Miss Virna nowhere! Just look at you, you cain't hardly stand let alone wheel this chair and I ain't been the length of that drive in years!'

'Trust me, Libby. Virna, will you come?'

'Can't say that I will, Richard. What Libby says is true, besides, this house is world enough for me and I don't trust outside. It's too sharp an' too wide.'

'Listen to me, Virna. Between us, Libby and myself, we can move the chair. Here Libby, help me turn it around.'

Libby is wild eyed and shaking. Her fingers are fluttering Virna's shawl until the whole room reeks of peppermint.

'C'mon girl, help me!'

'Libby. Don't you lift a finger!' Virna grasps the wheels of the chair firmly, 'And pray who's going to push me back up the hill when you two fools are plain wore out and fit for nothin'?'

'Trust me Virna. You won't need to come back. This is a beginning, remember?'

'What foolishness is this, Richard?'

'It's not foolishness, Virna. It's a beginning.'

'And where will it end this time, Richard? In a fool's tears again?'

'That's up to you Virna, it's your beginning.'

'And you've come all this time back to ask me to be a fool?'

'They say there's no fool like an old one. So start by acting your age. Come on Libby, help push this damn chair.'

Libby folds the shawl over Miss Virna's hands and takes up one side of the handles. Between them they steer the chair along Libby's path through the drawing room and into the hall. As they pass the card table, Virna drops the calling card onto the bare wood.

'I may choose to consider it... later.'

Between them, Richard and Libby tilt the chair across the threshold until they are clear of the porch.

Virna turns around in the chair, 'Libby. The door.'

Richard pushes hard on the handle and the wheels begin to roll, 'Leave it, Libby. Doors are for opening, not shutting.'

The chair is hard to push on the gravel, but by the time they reach the front of the house Libby has stopped shaking and is beginning to put some weight behind her side of the handle. They pause for a moment at the top of the drive to watch it curve away towards the church.

Virna pulls the shawl around her, 'So much world.'

'So many moon-apples.'

She looks up as Richard speaks, then allows her gaze to follow the continuing sweep of the drive to where the Station sits with white clouds spewing out from under the gables.

'Well... I may as well begin by being a fool, I been most other things. Libby? Hold tight girl!'

The chair slowly gathers speed down the drive. Richard and Libby hold it from running away as Virna sits, stony-faced and rigid, half afraid.

'Hold on a minute.'

Richard digs in a heel and applies the brake. The chair halts not twenty yards from the house. Libby is panting.

'It's alright, Mr Richard. I'm okay. 'fact my head's never been this quiet for as long as I remember.'

As they set off again, she notices that Richard's stoop has gone. Twenty yards further and she sees Miss Virna's shawl becoming pale and grey, like the clock pigeons, and that Mr Richard is standing straighter and his limp is now just a sometime stumble and that the air is warmer than it had been inside the house and that it still tasted like peppermint.

Virna's face is less lined now, but still immobile. The black fingerless lace gloves are now white and lay in her dark lap like a snowfall. By the time they near the church, Virna has her eyes closed and is showing the first faint trace of a smile.

'How are you at beginnings now, Virna?'

'Fine, Mr Clayburgh. Foolishly Fine!'

A few feet beyond the church, Virna asks them to stop.

'I think I might walk a step.'

'Then you'll be needing these.'

Richard pushes his hands into the hedgerow beside them and pulls out a handful of carmine satin and ribbon.

'My shoes! My dancin' shoes! Mr Clayburgh, for a gentleman you sure have a seductive way about you.'

'So you've begun to notice.'

Virna smiles openly at him.

'Libby! Help me put them on!'

Libby kneels down to take off Miss Virna's slippers before realising what she has done. She signs a cross over her breast, and admires the supple softness of her own knees as she laces and ties the ribbons. As Virna stands up from the chair the darkness slips from her clothes, leaving her bright and cautiously uncertain in the sunlight. She takes a step, wary at first, then one more. Suddenly, she skips. She stops herself and turns to laugh at Richard, but the old man is gone. The young man who stands there smiles down at her.

'Don't stop now, Virna. You've only just begun.'

'Begun what, Richard?'

'It doesn't matter Virna, it's just a beginning.' He jumps up, arms outstretched, 'Look, there's another! And there! Catch them on a breeze! Take them on the wing! They're yours.'

He links his arm through hers, 'Come on, we're late.'

Libby tags on behind, collecting summer flowers that pale against the print of her frock as Richard hurries them down to the Station.

Roy Jackson is waiting by the platform.

'Hi, Miss Virna, Mr Clayburgh.'

Libby hangs behind Virna and Richard, a flush taking her cheeks. She can't remember Roy ever being quite so handsome.

'Hello, Roy.'

'Why, hello Miss Libby. I can't tell you what a pleasure this is. And on such a fine day!'

Beside them the engine seethes in the heat of the afternoon. Steam escapes the pressure dome on top of the boiler and blasts upwards, swirling into the shade of the gable roof from where it appears again, swelling out like young clouds percolating through the gingerbread fascias.

Virna pays the engine no more than a cursory glance, 'I thought it was afire!'

Richard steers her away towards the first carriage.

'We're almost ready now, Roy.'

'Sure thing, Mr Richard.'

Roy steps up to the footplate, then stops to admire a show of long slender legs.

'See you later, Miss Libby?'

'You may be sure that I shall give it great consideration, Mr Jackson.'

Richard hands Libby up onto the train then turns to Virna, 'Almost forgot. I brought you this.'

From the inside pocket of his coat he offers her something slim and cellophaned with a golden ribbon around one end. Virna snatches it from him with glee.

'Why, Mr Clayburgh. Red-stripe candy. My very favourite.'

Richard lifts her into the carriage before staring back along the track. The engine that will take them onwards is as black as the absence of all light, but the blaze from the open firebox lights the mist of steam and the underside of the faded roof with a hopeful glow.

'Mr Jackson?'

Roy's hand lifts from the cab in reply.

Richard acknowledges it with an uncertain nod.

'I think we are ready.'

Hemmings wanders up the little side track by the church to find the old wheelchair unaccountably discarded in the drive. Without thinking too hard, he pushes it up towards the house. At the porch he finds the door swinging wide with the house empty and full of nothing but it's own echoes as usual.

Nothing seems to have been disturbed, and nothing seems to be missing... in fact, nothing much else, except for a strong scent of peppermint.

He steers the chair through to the lounge and sets it behind the half-opened shutter, beside Libby's old, grey-dusty, high-back carver chair, where it always was. From a lingering sense of loyalty he winds the old clock in the hall, then locks the door behind him to sit out on the bottom step.

His eyes close and his ears open to the day filtering the trees, the pipe soon warm in his hand. He pushes his heels out into the gravel of the drive, leans his back against the porch column and waits for his son to return, but Vietnam is nigh forty years gone now... he shrugs and tamps the pipe with his tobacco knife... and it's not wise to fill your house with too many ghosts.

Bryony Doran

is a prizewinning novelist, poet and consummate short story writer.

Her publications include:

'The China Bird', 2008
Winner of the Hookline Prize.

'The Sand Eggs', 2013
An intriguingly personal collection of short fiction based largely on her experiences as a stranger in a foreign land.

Bryony has also made several contributions to 'Matter' magazine, the Sheffield Hallam University MA anthology of short fiction.

Born in Devon and raised in Cornwall before moving north to York with her family, Bryony eventually settled in Sheffield where she met her partner, who is also a writer.

Bryony has one son, a serving soldier, and is currently engaged in the editing of her new pamphlet of poetry under the working title of 'Preparation for Theatre'. It explores the kaleidoscope of emotion that families faced while their children served in Afghanistan.

Suppose I was to tell you...

...that when I first came here to this country I arrived at Victoria Station in London and changed to another coach going to the north of England. It was full of people speaking my language. I had not expected this. I felt like one of those creatures in Norway who every year jumps off the cliff. I did not know the English name for these creatures.

I spoke to no one. I had come to this country to improve my English and get a good job. Every new word I learnt I put in my little black book my friend gave me. It had elastic around it and a hole along the back for a pencil. I looked out of the window at all the people and cars going around a big arch. It felt very exciting. I saw a sign that said Marble Arch. I wished I had stayed in London.

I was going to the city of Sheffield because my friend Anna was there, she said it was okay, cheaper than London and I could get somewhere to stay before I came.

I hoped there would be fields there so I would not miss my home so much, but there were no fields. It was a city of many hills and sometimes on the bus, if I sat upstairs, I could see fields far away. When I first came it was winter. When it became spring I liked the city better. I hadn't noticed before how many trees there were.

Anna said, if I didn't want to work in the sandwich factory with her, to get a bus to the richer part of the city and ask in the cafés. The advert for the waitress job was in a newsagent window next door to a café.

The advert said,
- *Waitress Wanted* and a phone number.

Next to it was another card
- *Wanted: Live in Cleaner, Child minder, and other general duties to be discussed.*

Anna said I had to be careful not to go anywhere on my own so I went into the shop and asked the newsagent about the waitress job. He was a nice man. He told me the café was right next door.

Agnes, the owner, who interviewed me, said my English was okay. Yes, I thought it is okay for a woman who wanted to be an English Teacher. You'll get £4.80 an hour she said, and tips, so you'll probably come out with about £5.

I didn't. People don't give big tips when you are serving them coffee and sandwiches, not in this country anyway. She did not ask me if I wanted the job but told me I could have it!

I would say that the newsagent man later became my friend. I was the one who would always go to get milk when we ran out. The other waitresses said he was pervy. I had to ask what they meant. They laughed at me and said you know – pervert. I had to ask them how to spell it and when I got home I looked it up in my dictionary. I think they were unkind. It was true he was always watching my bum but why in this country do women not like men looking at them? We had to wear tight black polyester trousers for work. Agnes told me where to buy them. They cost me £23, more than half a day's wages. I had to use some of my savings. My old boyfriend back in Poland, the one everyone thought I would marry until I found out I could come here, he said I had a nice bum. I always thought it was too big but he said men like bottoms like mine and I think he was right, not only because of the newsagent man but also the men that came into the café. Several times I was asked out. Would I like to go for a drink is how they said it. I just smiled and shook my head. Anna said I had to be careful of going out with English men, the Polish men in our house would get very angry and throw me out.

I liked working in the café even though the money wasn't good. My mother shouted at me when I phoned her after I got my first wage packet. She had heard that Anna got more in the sandwich factory. I lied and told her there were no jobs left there. I did not want to work with Polish people. I didn't tell her how much the rent was that I had to pay to the Polish man who owned our house, or that I shared a room with Anna and three other Polish women. My mother kept crying. She was very worried about our pope, John Paul. She had heard that he was unwell. She told me that every day she went to our church to pray for him.

The customers that came into the café were polite people. The English are polite people. I had not believed Anna when she'd told me these people said 'thank you' to the bus driver when they got off the bus, but it was true.

One of the waitresses, Becky, was kind to me, she laughed when I asked her the meaning of words, but she told me the answers.

Sometimes the customers were friendly. Often I got asked if I was French. I liked that, I knew I shouldn't and often I thought I should say yes, I am French, but something stopped me.

I am Polish I'd say. Oh, they'd say, and I'd see a look of boredom come into their eyes. Us Polish here in England, we are, how would you say it, the weeds, the new weeds that have blown in, we are the two a penny. We are all here.

After I had worked in the café for a few weeks I began to see the same people. Sometimes they would come every day at the same time or sometimes they would come every week, like one man who told me he came up from London. He was a lecturer at the university. I asked him questions about London. He asked me questions about my life before I came to this country. He asked me if I would like to go for a drink. I told him I didn't drink and he said that he thought all Polish people drank. I thought that was rude but later I thought I might say yes if he asked me again. I liked the way he dressed and his laugh. The only thing I missed about my boyfriend was the feeling of his skin against mine.

There was one woman who came in at nine o clock on Monday, Tuesday and Wednesday and then not again until the following Monday.

She always sat at the same table in the window. I think she liked the sun on her back. I used to watch for her coming in and if someone was sitting at her table she would have a creasing of skin between her eyebrows. Back then I did not know what the English word for this was. She was a woman with hair the colour of amber, even her eyebrows. Her skin was very pale, like a chicken before it is cooked. On top of the pale skin she had little brown spots on her face and on her arms. She could have been a pretty woman, but I never saw any men looking at her bottom. Somehow she didn't belong to her body. She was the only customer who ever asked me my name. I told her it was Klaudia and she said it was a lovely name and sounded like cloud. I looked this word up. I was not sure it was a good thing to have a name that sounded like cloud. I wanted to ask her what her name was but I didn't think I should, but then when I brought her skinny latte she told me.

Shirley, she said. I had to ask her what she meant. I had never heard this word before. She said, my name is Shirley. I wondered if Shirley would become my friend. Always she would read a newspaper for ten minutes and then she would get out some work from her briefcase and use a green pen to make notes. She would stay for two hours and drink two skinny lattes. The first time I served her, I had to ask one of the other waitresses what skinny meant.

Over the weeks I learnt more about Shirley. She was also a university lecturer. I asked her what her subject was and when she told me English, I told her that my dream had always been to do an English degree. She smiled then and asked me why didn't I turn my dream into a reality? She said she would find out for me if I could study in this country and she asked me what exams I had taken in Poland. I didn't think she meant to help me, but then the next week she brought me a glossy book all about the university. I still have it.

After I had been working in the café for two months, I think it would have been around the middle of March, it was still cold but there were flowers the colour of ripe plums in a concrete pot outside the newsagents. They looked like they had little faces. I saw in the window that the job...

—*Wanted: Live in Cleaner, child minder, and other general duties to be discussed.*

...was still there, after all this time. Every week when I phoned my mother she asked me if I had a better paid job yet. Every week she asked me if I have been to church to pray for John Paul.

The man in the newsagents said he knew the woman who put the advert in the window. She lived in one of the roads just off the high street. He said she was a nice woman, nice family, a Guardian family. He laughed then. I asked him what he meant. He said they had the Guardian newspaper delivered every day, and on a Sunday, The Observer. Didn't I know what sort of people read the Guardian? I shook my head and he pulled his lips together like a purse, they were thin lips, wavy like a child had drawn them.

'I suppose you could say they are socialists, well-off, educated socialists,' he said.

'In my country,' I said, 'it is the poor that are the socialists.'

He laughed, 'Yes, I suppose...' (he used that word a lot. I looked it up but I was still not sure of the meaning) '...you would think that. But you see it makes them feel good, being rich and supporting the poor.'

I wanted to know, do poor people read the Guardian?

He laughed again at that. 'Not many, love.' (I noticed he always called me love,) 'They can't afford the time.'

He came out from behind the counter; I wondered what he was going to do. I knew he had a wife, a woman who wore a flowery overall.

'If you are interested in that job...' He leaned into the window. I watched his bottom then. It was a flat bottom in cheap grey trousers. I thought, why he always wears dark jumpers? On each shoulder was that stuff that falls from your hair. I wondered what the English word for it was. I suppose I could have asked him. If he'd worn a grey jumper to match his grey trousers and his grey hair no one would have known of his problem.

He handed me the card, 'Take it, she hasn't paid me for two weeks anyway. And if you want the job it'll stop anyone else getting it.'

It's funny what you notice once someone has told you something. All that day I looked at the newspapers the customers were reading, and he was right. The same sort of people were reading the same papers. The Guardian readers, they looked educated, but weren't smartly dressed. Two asked for decaffe coffee.

I thought, the man from London, and Shirley, I think they must read the Guardian newspaper.

I didn't want to leave my job. I was finding out a lot about the English and I think my English was improving but I knew my mother was right, I had to earn more money. If I could send enough money home to keep her quiet and save some, I might one day be able to study. Shirley had checked my qualifications and said she thought I could study here.

Anna again mentioned the job in the sandwich factory but I told her I had found out about a job with a good family. If they were good people I would get a good wage and maybe if the hours were shorter I would be able to take a bus and go out into the country.

After work that night I found a phone box that was working and rang the number on the card. A man answered. I told him why I was ringing but he didn't seem very interested.

He said, 'I'll get my wife.' I heard him walking through the house. I remember thinking they must have wooden floors.

'Hello. Yes, can I help you?'

A funny question to ask, I thought.

'I was ringing about the advertisement you put in the newsagent's window for a cleaner and child minder.'

'Is that Klaudia? The girl from the café?'

I did not understand how she knew my name.

'It's Shirley here – what a coincidence.'

I went to her house the next evening. The clocks had just gone back. That is what they say in this country. It was March and suddenly there was another hour of sunlight in the evening. I wanted to go to see Shirley straight after work, it would have been better for me, I wouldn't have to pay two bus fares, but no, she said, it wasn't convenient. So I had to go back to my house on the bus. It was better anyway. It gave me a chance to wash and change.

I put on my black skirt and coiled my hair up at the back of my head.

She took me to the kitchen at the back of the house. As we passed through the hall I saw her husband sitting on a white leather sofa watching a big television. He had a glass of white wine in his hand. He had long hair and an old face.

Shirley asked me to be quiet for a minute, putting a finger up to her lips, then she pointed to me to sit at the table. She was listening to something on the radio, voices, and then music started and she switched the radio off and picked up the kettle and took it over to the sink.

At least she was hospitable. That was a good sign. I had heard that English people weren't hospitable. But Shirley was a kind person so I should have known that anyway.

'Just getting my daily fix of The Archers,' she said, 'Of course you can't ever have heard of The Archers, it's a very English thing.'

She didn't explain any further so I had to wait until I got home to look the word up, and I was still none the wiser – as the English say. Why would she think a person expert in the use of bow and arrow is such an English thing?

She offered me a coffee. She made it in a cafetière. I noticed when she was making the coffee that she was quite slim except for her hips. She wore a skirt in a heavy brown cloth and around the broadest part of her hips, down the back below the zip, the stitches had come apart. The coffee was good. She kept looking at me and smiling, 'You look younger somehow.'

I told her I was twenty-eight, she said she was surprised.

I could hear voices of children coming from upstairs. I had never thought of Shirley with children.

She sat down opposite me, holding her mug like a baby would a bottle, grasping it tight with both hands.

'I haven't really thought this through. I've had a few people apply but none of them were suitable. But you!'

She smiled at me then. She had a nice smile and I remembered why I had liked her. Somehow in her home she seemed different.

She asked me how much I was getting in the café. I thought it was rude but I told her and she made this funny sucking in sound as if she had burnt her finger.

'That's a bit expensive. If you lived in that would make it a lot cheaper for you wouldn't it? And I could help you with your studies, couldn't I?'

I nodded. I didn't know what to say.

'I could pay you say, £3 an hour and you'd still be a lot better off wouldn't you?'

I used the newsagents word then – 'I suppose... but. Yes, well, I don't think, excuse me for saying, but I don't think £3 is the minimum wage.'

I saw the crease appear again between her eyes.

'Are you legal here?'

I nodded.

'Oh, but,' she clapped her hands together, '...it won't apply will it? You'll be getting board and lodgings.'

'I would be working full time?'

'Yes, I need someone to look after my daughter, she's eighteen months, and do all the household duties of course. God, it will be such a relief. When can you start?'

I added up the numbers is my head. If I didn't have to pay for my food or rent or bus fares I would have just a little more money, maybe I could do some overtime too, and I could begin my studies with Shirley's help. I wondered if I could trust this woman, but then I remembered what the newsagent man had said.

When I told the man from London I was leaving he asked me for my number. I told him I didn't have one. What about email? I had to explain that my email address was in the Polish language. He gave me his card. He was a professor of English.

When I am no longer in the house of a Polish man, I thought, I will be able to go out with English men.

Becky gave me a hug when I told her I was leaving. She said she was going to miss me. I hadn't realised how much I liked Becky until she did that. I think you could almost say we were friends. She said we must get that pint in before you leave and so the day before I left, after work, we went to a pub a few doors away from the café.

It was the first time I had been in an English pub and I liked it, everyone was friendly to us and said hello. We were the only women in the pub. There were men at the bar in work clothes, as if they had been working on a building site all day. I felt a little shy but Becky pushed through to the bar and asked me what I wanted to drink. I didn't know what to say so I asked for the same drink as she was having.

One of the men said to me, 'You're not from around here are you?' Which seemed like an odd question, though I was polite and answered him, 'No.'

Becky got out a packet of cigarettes and asked me if I wanted one. There was an ashtray on the table made of green glass. It was empty except for one smoked cigarette. Becky asked me about my new job and I told her about it and how Shirley was going to help me to study. She asked me if I was sure it was all Kosher. I explained I hadn't asked whether the family were Jewish. She started laughing at this, laughing and laughing, making me laugh too, though I didn't know what I was laughing at. The men at the bar looked over at us and raised their glasses. Becky had got me a large glass of pale beer. I liked it.

'We use Kosher to mean, is something legitimate. Is it a proper job,' she explained, wiping her eyes.

'She is paying me money if that is what you mean?'

'Do you know how much, how many hours and who's going to pay your tax and National Insurance? You won't get your old job back. Agnes is pretty pissed off at you, I heard her grumbling about all the bother she'd gone to, to get you a work certificate. Mind you, that's not stopped her employing another Pole.'

'She is an educated English woman, a university lecturer,' I explained, 'She will know all this.'

Becky made a noise like a startled horse blowing through its nose, 'Seriously, you need to check these things out. You could end up not getting any benefits or not being able to study here. You could even end up getting sent back. And if you want to do a degree you need to start soon, the fees go up to £3,000 next year.'

'Don't worry,' I told her, 'It will be alright. Shirley has promised to help me with my studies. She is a good woman. A Guardian reader!'

That started her laughing again. I don't know why but I started laughing too. One of the men from the bar brought us two glasses of the same beer. He didn't try to sit down with us or talk to us. He just put the beer down and smiled and went away. When I stopped laughing I asked Becky should I go to the bar to pay for the beer but she shook her head and raised her glass and shouted, 'thanks,' over to the men. They raised their glasses. I couldn't remember the last time I had been so happy.

My evening with Becky I enjoyed very much. I wish I could learn to tell when she is joking at me. I found out that she has a degree in philosophy. I wanted to ask why she was working in a café but I thought it would be rude. I learnt many English words that evening. This is the reason I change my job. I shall learn much English and study with Shirley.

On the first day of my new job I had to get a much earlier bus. The people standing at the bus stop were not the people I usually saw. My suitcase was very heavy and a nice man helped me onto the bus with it.

As the bus went along the dual carriageway I saw bunches of daffodils. This should have made me feel happy but it did not. On Saturday our Pope had died. We were all so happy when a Polish Pope was chosen. The world woke up to Poland, and now he is dead.

We did not have a television in our house. Pavel, one of the Polish men, told me the news and on Sunday I went to the newsagents near our house and asked for a Guardian. The man laughed at me and said there was no Guardian on a Sunday. He suggested I get The Observer. It was very heavy when I picked it up. There was a picture of John Paul II on the front. He had a very kind face our Polish Pope, and now he was dead. I forgot to look at how much the paper was and when the man asked me for the money it was nearly half an hour of my wages. I said that I was sorry but that I could not afford it and he was very nasty and said, You mean you've already read what you want. Bloody Polacks. It was the first time I had cried in this country. This man was an immigrant too, I could tell by the colour of his skin. Why would he be so unkind to me?

When I arrived at the house, Shirley's husband answered the door. His name was Peter. We have this name in my country. It is a biblical name. He shook my hand. His hand was damp and soft like a woman's. He was wearing a beige suit and already, early in the morning, it looked as if it needed ironing. I think this fabric is linen.

He said that Shirl was in the shower.

I didn't know what to do. I could see the children through the door, the baby girl and a little boy of about five. They were watching the TV. They still had on the clothes they slept in.

When they are all out, I thought, I shall put on the TV to hear about John Paul.

Peter's hair was like the colour of a hay field. The children had red hair like their mother. I wondered why an old man should have long hair. I asked him if he was an artist and he laughed. Why do these English people always laugh?

'Media studies,' he said, 'I suppose,' – that word again – 'you could call me an artist.'

I heard Shirley coming down the stairs. She was dressed. She had trousers on in the same fabric as Peter's suit and they were creased too. Her hair was still wet from the shower. She looked at me and again there was a frown between her eyebrows (I had asked Becky for the word).

She didn't say, 'Hello Klaudia,' but, 'Oh, you're here.'

I thought this was an odd thing to say and I got the feeling that she wished I wasn't.

'Have the kids had their breakfast?'

I was not sure who she was asking. She asked the kids. They said, 'No.'

'And they're not even dressed. For Christ's sake Pete, couldn't you have been giving Claudia some instructions?'

Then she noticed my suitcase, 'I'm sorry, everything gets a bit chaotic round here in the morning, come through to the kitchen and I'll give you some instructions for today.'

The children had breakfast out of a packet that said Coco Pops. They ate it in front of the TV. Shirley told me their names were Chloe and James.

I walked to school with Shirley's friend, Penny. She also had two children the same age as Shirley's. She was what Becky called a 'yummy mummy.' I recognized her from the café but she didn't recognize me. The women she came to the cafe with were very messy. We had to clear up after their children. A bloody bombsite, Becky used to say.

I was glad Chloe was in her pram. I did not like the way English people let their very small children run along the pavement. That morning the traffic was not moving. I think the English name for this is rush hour. I did not want to talk to Penny, as I was anxious about watching James running ahead, so I just listened.

'Shirl is so lucky having an au pair. I wish I could afford one. I don't know how they're going to pay you though, with the mortgage they've got.'

I don't think Penny liked Shirley very much.

At the school gates she asked me if I could do any babysitting for her. I didn't know what to say so I tried.

'I suppose so.'

'You suppose? What do you mean, suppose?'

I must have got the meaning wrong, I thought.

'You either can or you're can't.'

I didn't know what to say. I was not sure about the word au pair. I made a note to look it up and hoped Shirley had a good dictionary.

I put the key in the lock. It was a pale gold key with Chubb written on it. I was glad there were no cars on the drive. The television was still on. Chloe went to sit in front of it. I made myself a cafetière and some toast and butter. It felt very strange doing this in someone else's house. Shirley had left me some books to look at from the University. I thought about what Becky had said about the tuition fees going up. I had to start my degree before this happened.

I walked through the house into each room. Shirley and Peter had a double bed and their own private bathroom.

At the top of the house there were two small rooms, offices, one was Shirley's and one Peter's. Doctor Shirley Mason, it said, on a university letter. She must be an important person I thought. There were dictionaries too heavy to take down with one hand. I looked up the word Au pair. But I was still not sure what it meant.

I tried to find the room where I was going to sleep. There wasn't one. The children had a room each so I supposed that Shirley would put them in one room. I would have liked to unpack my things.

On the kitchen table there was a long list of shopping to get from the supermarket. I read down the list. I saw the word polish and wondered did Shirley mean me to get Polish sausage. I shall have to do two trips I thought. But there was no money. How should I pay?

I hoped Chloe would have a sleep so I could change the TV channel and watch the news about our Pope but all she wanted to do was watch the TV, even in the afternoon she did not sleep.

The little boy did not like me very much; when I walked back from the school with him he made a joke of my accent – 'Please to come here.'

When we arrived to the house I was surprised to see, so early, two cars on the drive and the door wide open. Peter and Shirley were in the kitchen. He had the fridge door open.

He didn't say, 'Hello Klaudia,' but, 'Where's the beer?'

This man, he had the face of a peasant – like a potato. He pointed to the list on the table.

'Shirl did not leave me any money.'

I had said something wrong. I could see it in her face, but he started laughing. I don't know why.

'Shirl is it now, hmm?'

Shirley talked to me like Agnes used to. 'Surely you've got a credit card?'

This woman must have thought I was rich. I shook my head. I saw then she was sorry.

'This is going to take a bit more sorting out than I thought. I've got so much on my plate at the moment I haven't had time to think things through.'

I saw there was no plate in front of her and I remember thinking this must be an expression I do not know.

'Right, what shall we have for tea?' She looked in the fridge and then the freezer below and pulled out some frozen pizzas. 'Will you be eating with us before you get off?'

I did not understand what she was saying. I no longer had my bed at the Polish house. I noticed my English always was not good if I was upset – when I needed it to be good.

'I have brought my suitcase.'

'Oh God, of course you have.' She patted me on the arm, 'I'd forgotten all about you moving in.'

'Please where am I to sleep?'

'I was thinking about that the evening you came round for the job. Come with me.' She took me upstairs and showed me a couch at the top of the stairs. 'This is a bed settee, I've got a screen in the cellar – it'll be perfect. This is where our guests sleep.'

She helped me pull out the bed and explained I would have to put it away every day. I think she knew I was not happy and I saw it worried her.

'If you remind me later I'll send you some course links so you can have a look at what doing an English degree actually entails.'

Links! I did not understand. She saw I was confused.

'Let me have your email address.'

I understood then. I told her I did not have a computer and asked if she would mind if I used hers. She said for security reasons this was not possible.

On the Friday at the end of my first week, the funeral of John Paul II was on the TV. I did not care if Chloe cried. I had to watch John Paul's funeral. Maybe I could work out how to switch James' game machine on, and she would be happy with that but, when we got back to the house, Shirl's car was still on the drive. I had to watch the funeral. I would have to be brave and ask her. She was sitting at the kitchen table reading the Guardian, drinking her latte. At home she did not drink skinny latte.

She looked up and smiled, 'I'm working from home today.'

I had to ask her. 'Would you mind very much if I watched the funeral of John Paul?'

'Who?'

'The Pope!'

'What about Chloe's programs?'

'It is my duty. I have to pay my respects. He is our Pope.'

'Are you religious?'

Why do the English always ask this, as if it is something I have a choice about.

'Well okay, but I want you to babysit for me tonight.'

I felt strange sitting on the white sofa. It was the first time I had sat there. I would have liked a cup of coffee but somehow it did not feel right.

There were many people in the square in Rome. Three or four million the newsman said. All to honour our Polish Pope in his red robe. I thought of my mother and I cried. Sometimes I missed my country.

Peter and Shirley drank a bottle of red wine before they went out. They did not offer me a glass. Shirley looked very nice. She had a shiny dress on. Peter still had on his linen suit.

They came to stand in the kitchen doorway. I was washing the dishes.

'Not sure when we'll be back,' Peter laughed. 'But I don't suppose it matters.'

Shirl smiled, 'It'll give you a chance to do some studying,'

'Please, before you go, can I have my wages?'

They both looked at each other and laughed. 'Wages!'

I was not sure if I had used the right word?

Shirl laughed. 'You've only been here five days.'

'At the café I got paid every week. I have to send money home. My family are poor.'

'I'm really sorry, but you'll get paid monthly. I can't possibly afford to pay you weekly. We'd have to dip into our savings.'

'How am I going to manage without any money?'

'You haven't got any expenses, you'll be fine, I suppose I could always loan you a small amount in advance. Let me have your bank details tomorrow and I'll pay your wages in at the end of the month, after I've been paid.'

I took off the blue rubber gloves I bought with my own money. 'I do not have a bank account.'

They looked at each other and laughed. I did not find this funny.

'No bank account!' They said it both at the same time.

'We'll have to remedy that, won't we?' Shirl said.

I remembered what Becky had said and followed them to the front door.

'You will give me a wage slip showing my National Insurance payments and tax, won't you?'

They looked at each other like puppets in a children's show. These people were drunk. I should have asked these things earlier.

'My dear girl,' Peter shook his first finger at me. 'What do you expect? We're not the council. We're not employers.'

I did not understand what he meant. He shut the door in my face.

They woke me up when they came in. They were very drunk. I heard them having sex. It made me feel lonely. They went into their bathroom. They were laughing.

'National Insurance – what planet is she on?'

He was urinating. 'How much are you paying her?'

I did not hear Shirl's reply but I heard him say, 'Bloody hell, we're going to be quids in.'

In the morning I thought I shall look up this word. I said it over and over to myself so I wouldn't forget it. Quidsin, quidsin, quidsin...

The word was not in my small dictionary. On Monday I looked it up in Shirl's big dictionary. I turned all the pages for 'Q' but I could not find the word.

On her next day off Shirl took me to the bank and helped me open an account and paid £30 in to it as a loan. I said thank you, but I was not sure if I meant it.

At the end of April as promised my wages were paid into my new account. I had to go to the bank to see how much my wages were. They were not as much as I had expected. Shirl was helping me with my studies so I did not say anything. In the evening, when the children were asleep, I went to an Internet café and looked up the links she sent me. I also emailed the London man. I wondered if I would get a reply.

Shirl said that when the exams were over and she was less busy, she would arrange an interview for me at the university. To tell the truth I was not very happy in my new job but the thought of the interview helped me to keep going. I supposed it would all work out as it was supposed to in the end, and my English was improving every day?

The 7th of July was my birthday. I had not told anyone. I had been with Shirl for three and a half months. I liked England in the summer. Shirl's garden had many beautiful flowers. It was one of my jobs to look after them.

On the way back from school that morning I went to the newsagent. Peter had asked me to pay the paper bill as they had received a nasty letter. He had given me a cheque. I had not seen the newsagent man or been in the café since I started my new job.

The newsagent man was pleased to see me and asked if I liked my new job? I did not know what to say. He looked surprised.

'I am not sure,' I said, 'if they are good people.'

He frowned then, 'How do you mean?'

I had to wait a minute before I replied. I wanted to cry.

'You said they were socialists. Socialists are supposed to look after poor people.'

He laughed then, not just a bit, but so much that he had to hold on to the edge of his counter, I saw his belly moving up and down under his shirt.

'I forgot the word that should go before socialist: Pseudo.'

I had never heard this word before.

'They play at it like kids,' he said.

I did not understand what he meant so when I got back to the house I put Chloe in front of the TV. The sound was turned off and there was a News channel on with lots of fire engines flashing blue lights and a bus with its top blown off. I did not stay to see what was happening but ran upstairs to Shirl's room and got down her big dictionary, and turned the pages to 'S'.

Caroline Pitcher

Caroline's childhood was spent mostly out-of-doors in East Yorkshire, near Hull. Then and now, much of her writing is concerned with the relationship between people and the natural world. This is especially true in her finely illustrated stories for younger children, such as 'The Time of the Lion', 'The Littlest Owl', 'Nico's Octopus', 'Time for Bed, Little One' (read on CBeebies by Charlie Condou), 'Lord of the Forest', 'The Snow Whale' (shortlisted for the Children's Book Award) and 'Home, Sweet Home', whose protagonist is a frog.

'Kevin the Blue', the Independent Story of the Year, is about a boy and a kingfisher, and the quartet 'The Shaman Boy' tells the story of brothers in a war-torn land. Its first novel, 'Cloud Cat', is about a snow leopard, and gained an East Midlands Writer's Award.

Other published titles are 'Ghost in the Glass', 'The Dolphin Bracelet' and various stories in anthologies.

On leaving University of Warwick, having had a wonderful three years reading English and European Literature, she worked in a Hull fish factory, on adding machines in an office, as the assistant in a Mayfair art gallery, and then as a teacher in East London for eleven years. 'Diamond', her first novel, was set here. It won the Kathleen Fidler Award.

Caroline enjoys talking at festivals, being a visiting author in schools and writing with children and adults.

Her young adult novels, '11 o'clock Chocolate Cake', 'Mine', and 'Silkscreen' are reprinted in 2014 by Cybermouse Multimedia Ltd. and are available from bookshops.

Mariana and The Merchild

An old woman lived alone in a ramshackle hut by the sea. Her name was Mariana.

Whenever Mariana walked on the shore, the village children stole after her, pulling faces. She longed for them to be her friends but, if she turned around, they ran.

The sea looked after Mariana as if it was her mother. It brought her fish to eat and wood to burn. She loved to listen to its music as it boomed and crashed and sucked pebbles from the shore, but sometimes it filled her with fear. You see, deep in the sea caves and forests there hid hungry sea-wolves, waiting for a storm.

When the storm came, it was terrible. The winds tore at the hut and tugged at the roof. The sea-wolves threw back their heads ands howled and out they came. All night they prowled along the shore, baying in the wind and rain. And all night Mariana trembled in the corner of her ramshackle hut with her hands clapped tight over her ears.

Towards dawn, the winds tired and the sea-wolves crept back into their underwater caves.

Mariana tiptoed to the door.

The storm had blown the sky clear of clouds and the sunlight dazzled her, bright as a burst mirror. The sea was surging as if a volcano had thrown out jewels of turquoise and indigo, aquamarine and emerald. Mariana stood in the warmth to soothe her rickety-rackety bones and saw that the sea had brought her wood and fish.

'There's plenty!' she cried. 'I could cook for the children too, if they'd let me.'

She knelt by a rock pool as clear as glass. It was full of treasures brought by the sea; ruby anemones, a shell like a sunburst, a silver sea horse and a golden starfish. In the middle, half-hidden by seaweed, lay a crab as fine as a shield. Mariana lifted it into her basket and collected seaweed and driftwood for her fire. She struggled back to her hut, put the basket on the table and lifted up the seaweed.

'Why, what's this?' she cried, for the crab had split in two.

Inside lay a baby girl, with hair the colour of the setting sun, skin that gleamed like a rosy pearl and a fish's tail with scales of blue and silver.

'Look what the sea has brought me!' cried Mariana, and at once she loved that baby more than she had ever loved anything.

She carried the baby in its crab-shell cradle to the village and took her to the Wise Woman's house.

For a long time the Wise Woman was silent. When she spoke, her voice trembled. 'This is a Merbaby. Her mother hid her in the crab-shell to keep her safe from the sea-wolves.'

'I must let her mother know she is safe,' said Mariana. 'Who is she?'

'A Sea Spirit,' whispered the Wise Woman. 'Take care, Mariana. Put the Merbaby safely out of reach of the sea-wolves and hide yourself away to watch what happens.'

Mariana went back to the shore and set the crab-shell cradle high on a rock. She smiled down at the Merbaby and said, 'You're not afraid of me like the village children, are you?' and the Merbaby smiled back.

Mariana hid herself away to watch. She was just about to fall asleep in the sun when she heard someone singing, but not words from this world.

Seven great waves came rolling into shore, waves of crimson and rose and gold, and on the seventh rode the Sea Spirit.

She was as tall as a mast. Her hair flamed red and her skin shone as if it was mother-of-pearl polished by the sun. All the colours of the rainbow shimmered in her fish's tail.

Her opal eyes lit upon the crab-shell cradle. She picked up her Merbaby and began to sing a lullaby, but not of this world, and her voice sighed like the far-away pull of the sea.

Mariana cried, 'I didn't mean to steal your baby. I thought the sea had brought her for me.'

The Sea Spirit looked at Mariana. Her eyes flickered, no colour and every colour. She sang, 'The sea did bring her for you, Mariana. I hid my baby inside the shell to keep her from the sea-wolves, but the storm swept the cradle away. You have saved her life. Look after her for me now, until the seas lie calm. I will come every day to feed her and teach her how to swim.'

So Mariana and the Merchild lived together in the ramshackle hut, safe from the restless sea. It was the happiest time of the old woman's life.

The Merchild grew stronger and her hair grew longer, burnished red as the setting sun. She liked to lie in the shallow waves and watch the shells open and close like mouths. She laughed as she watched the village children run along the shore after the sea-birds and jump from rock to rock. They peeped over the rocks at Mariana and the Merchild and no longer ran away when the old lady smiled at them.

The Merchild liked to watch Mariana's fire spangle her tail with pink and vermilion, and she learned to speak the words of our world. When she sang, her voice was like the echo of the sea inside a shell, and Mariana loved her so.

Every day the Sea Sprit rode in on the seventh wave. She fed the Merchild and taught her to swim, first in the sheltered rock pool and then further out to sea.

'Dear Merchild,' whispered Mariana. 'I dread the time when you must return to the sea.'

Mariana walked on the shore and thought, 'If I kept the Merchild shut in the hut, the Sea Spirit could not take her from me.' She went back to her hut, where the Merchild was making necklaces of shells for the village children. She looked up and smiled, and Mariana's heart felt as if it would melt. She thought, 'No... the Merchild is from the sea. I must let her return, even though I will be alone again.'

She turned to the children and asked, 'Shall I cook you all something to eat?' They looked at each other. 'Yes please!' they said.

At last came the morning Mariana was dreading.

The Sea Spirit sang, 'My child can swim and it is time to take her home. The sea is calm and the sea-wolves cannot catch her. We will never forget you, Mariana.'

The Sea Spirit took her Merchild on her back, far out to sea, while Mariana stood with tears streaming down her face.

The children stole up behind Mariana. They took her hands and comforted her.

But the Merchild had not gone forever. Each morning she leapt from the waves to greet Mariana and once she brought her a lustrous pearl from the sea-bed.

The Sea Spirit sent in waves brimful of fish, and the rock pools teemed with shrimps and crabs and sea-weed.

When a storm was coming Mariana heard the sea-wolves whimpering, but she was no longer afraid of them.

And these days the children helped Mariana carry her wood and food home, and they often stayed for tea.

Danuta Reah

grew up with stories. Her father, a Polish cavalry officer who escaped the Nazi invasion and joined the Polish Free Forces in the UK, kept his past alive by telling his children stories of his own childhood in the forests of Poland and Belarus.

Her successful crime debut in 1999 with 'Only Darkness' was followed by 'Silent Playgrounds', 'Night Angels', and 'Bleak Water', all set against a vivid South Yorkshire urban back-drop.

Her subsequent novels, 'The Forest of Souls', set in war-torn Belarus, and 'Strangers', with an expatriate Saudi Arabian background, (written as 'Carla Banks') took her work onto an International Stage including; USA, Netherlands, the Nordic countries and most of central and eastern Europe.

Her dark, psychological books explore the issues that confront urban society: family breakdown, migration, and the distortions of the justice system, through the context of the modern crime novel.

In 2005 Danuta won the CWA Short Story Dagger Award with 'No Flies on Frank', against established competition.

Her work as a University Lecturer in Linguistics, plus her research into links between language disorders and criminal behaviour, has led to work in the field of forensic linguistics. Danuta's publications include several text books.

Her latest novel, 'The Last Room', written as Danuta Reah, was published in June 2014. She is currently working on a non-fiction book about Jack the Ripper.

Danuta lives in South Yorkshire with her husband, who is an artist.

Out of Her Mind

Words on a page, black print on white. Words on a screen, black print on a flickering monitor, safe, contained. He's the shadow in the night, the soft footsteps that follow in the darkness, sealed away as the book is closed, fragmenting into nothing as the screen shuts down into blackness.

But now he's seeping around the sides of the screen, bleeding off the edges of the paper...

The room is empty. The light reflects from the walls, glints on the metal of the lamp. The screensaver dances, flowers and butterflies, over and over.

The summer heat was oppressive. Laura looked out of her window. The small patch of ground behind the house was scorched and wilting and, over the fence, the buddleia that grew in the alleyway drooped, its purple flowers brown at the tips.

The air was still and dry. The louvres were open, but the wind chimes she had put there at the beginning of the summer hung motionless. She tapped them with her finger, the gentle reverberation giving her the illusion of coolness.

'You going to sit there all day?'

Laura jumped and turned round quickly. It was David.

'You going to be sitting in front of that thing all day?' He resented the hours she spent in front of the screen.

'I was just...' She gestured towards the monitor where the screen saver danced in a pattern of butterflies. 'It won't come right. I need to...' She couldn't explain, but she knew she needed to keep on writing.

He was impatient. 'It's beautiful out there. I'm not going to be stuck in on a day like this. I'm going out. Are you coming?'

She looked round the room. Her study was stark with its north facing window and bare walls. Her desk was tucked away in a corner. It was quiet. It used to be safe.

'I have to go on. I can't leave it now.'

And she couldn't.

'You aren't doing anything. You're just staring out of the window. Can't you make an effort, pretend you want my company once in a while? I might as well be married to a machine.'

He was angry and frustrated. It was summer, a glorious summer's day, and Laura just wanted to sit in her study, staring at the white flicker of the screen, tap tapping her fantasy world into its electronic soul.

You married a writer, she wanted to say. That was the deal. But there was no point. He didn't want to hear it.

'I'm going.' He slammed out of the room, out of the house, doors opening and closing with noisy violence.

Laura let the silence close in on her, then turned back to her desk. Her hand hovered over the mouse for a second, then she pushed it, and the screen saver cleared.

Writing running down the screen. Just words on a page. And then a sound when the house is empty, a footstep in the corridor, the creak of someone outside the door.

It's nothing. It's imagination. He's always been there, the monster under the bed, the ogre in the cellar. Just a shadow to frighten children in the night.

Only, the footsteps are gone now. There is no monster under the bed, no ogre in the cellar. He used to live in Laura's mind, live on her screen, in the pages she writes. He used to hide behind the butterflies and the flowers of the screensaver. But now he's gone. He's escaped. He's somewhere else.

The butterflies used to dance on the buddleia, but now the flowers are dying and the butterflies have gone.

Laura was in the supermarket. She had decided to surprise David.

Look, I did the shopping!

He hated shopping. She took stuff off the shelves mechanically and loaded it into the trolley, bags of salad, bread, eggs, milk, bacon.

The supermarket aisles were long and well lit with rows of shiny tins and boxes reflecting the light into her eyes. Reds and yellows and greens, primary colours, nursery colours. The trolley had a red plastic handle and bars of aluminium and the boxes and bottles and tins on the shelves flickered as the bars ran past them, like the flicker of the words on the screen. She could see the patterns on the screensaver moving and dancing. Waiting.

She shouldn't have left. She had to hurry, she had to get back.

The aisles were long and straight. Laura pushed the trolley faster and faster past each one. Biscuits and cakes. Tinned fruit and vegetables. Soaps and cleaning stuff.

And a movement at the far end of the aisle.

She squinted but the light reflected off the tins and the bottles, reflected off the shiny floor. She screwed her eyes up, but she couldn't see it properly. It had been just a flicker, a silhouette moving quickly round the corner, out of view, out of sight.

She pushed her trolley into the next aisle, and her foot slipped in something sticky, something viscous, something that had spattered across the shelves and dripped onto the floor, red, dark, drip, drip, pooling round her feet in abstract patterns.

She stopped, frozen, half-hearing the voices: 'Look out, someone's dropped a bottle of wine... better be careful... mind the glass.... get a...'

She pushed past, the wheels of her trolley smearing through the red and leaving a trail on the floor behind her.

'Hey!' But the voices didn't matter. She had to get back.

The queue snaked away from the checkout. She pushed her trolley to the front. 'Sorry, so sorry...' as people stepped back, frowning, puzzled, too polite to object. She didn't have time to queue. She fed her purchases through and dug in her bag for her purse as the checkout girl drummed her fingers on the till and the queue stirred restlessly behind her.

'...with a filleting knife.'

She blinked. It was the girl sitting at the till, her face hostile and blank. 'What?'

'Forty five. Forty five pounds... Did he slash her?'

'What?'

The eyes rolled in exasperation. 'D'you want any cash back?'

'Oh. No.'

The car park dazzled in the sun, the concrete hot under her feet, the metallic paint of the cars sending shards of light into her eyes.

Night-time. He walks the streets. He waits in the dark places. A silk scarf whispers between his fingers. It's light and gauzy, patterned with flowers and butterflies. It's smooth and strong. He has something else in his hand. It's long and thin and sharp. It glints where the light catches it.

Someone is coming. The sound drifts around the roadway, loses itself in the darkness, in the wind that rustles the tops of the trees. It's what he's been waiting for, tap, tap, the sound of heels on the pavement, like the sound of fingers on a keyboard, like the sound of knuckles against the door. Tap, tap, tap. And then there will be the other sound, the sound that only the two of them will hear, the sound behind her in the darkness …the soft fall of footsteps, almost silent, lifted and placed carefully but quickly, moving through the night.

The heatwave broke two days later. In the morning the sky was cloudless, the shadows sharp as a knife on the walls and on the pavements. The buddleia, parched, drooped down, the petals falling into the dust.

Laura sat at the table crumbling a piece of toast between her fingers. The sun reflected off the polished surfaces of steel, off the cutlery, the spoons, the knives.

David sat opposite her, immersed in the paper he held up in front of his face. Laura stared at the print, black on white, words that would blur and vanish behind the moving patterns of flowers and butterflies.

'Maniac.' David closed the paper and tossed it onto the table.

Laura looked at the crumpled sheets.

WOMAN …KNIFE ATTACK.

She grabbed it and smoothed the page out, her hands moving in frantic haste.

WOMAN KILLED IN KNIFE ATTACK.

It had been the previous night, in the car park, in the supermarket car park. The woman must have walked across concrete that was still warm from the sun, her heels tapping briskly, the streetlights shining on her hair. Walking tap, tap, tap towards the shadows where the trees started, the trees that whispered in the night.

She went to her room and switched on her machine. Her hands hovered over the keyboard and then began to move. Tap, tap, tap. The words appeared on the screen, filled it, scrolled down and down as her hands flew over the keys.

She wrote and deleted, wrote and deleted, and each time, a woman walked into the darkness where gauze and flowers and butterflies fluttered in the wind. And the light glinted on something in the shadows, just for a moment.

The day greyed over as the clouds rolled in. The air cooled, became chill. Laura typed, deleted, typed again.

'Still at it? You've been here all day.'

She jumped and turned round.

It was David trying hard to be patient. 'I've made tea.'

'Thanks.' She wasn't hungry, but... 'Thanks.'

He'd made egg and chips. The chips lay pale and limp on the plate. The yolk of the egg trembled under its translucent membrane. She cut the chips into small pieces, pushed them into the egg, watched the bright yellow spill and spread over her plate.

'Egg and chips not good enough for you any more?'

He was angry again. He'd made the effort and she didn't appreciate it – didn't appreciate him.

She couldn't explain. She couldn't tell him.

'It's fine. Egg and chips is fine. I'm just not hungry, that's all.'

He grunted, but didn't say anything. He was trying. He was making the effort. He shook the sauce bottle over his plate. Smack as he hit the base with the flat of his hand. She watched red spatter over the mountain of chips.

'Ketchup?'

She shook her head. 'Did you get a paper? Is there any more about...?' About the murder.

'No. Stupid cow, though. What did she expect, out on her own at that time?'

What had she expected? She saw the wine spilled on the supermarket floor, the drip, drip from the shelves, the bright red of the splashes. David lifted a chip to his mouth.

Ketchup dropped onto the table, splat.

She had to get back.

The dark footprints cross the paving stones of the alleyway, prints that look black and shiny in the moonlight, growing fainter and fainter with each step until they fade to nothing.

It is starting to rain. The drops make black marks on the dry flags. The drops are big and heavy, splashing out as the rain falls harder and harder. The footsteps begin to blur, and a darker colour trickles across the ground with the rain that starts to run across the path, across the alleyway, running into a black pool that gleams in the shadows. And the puddles cloud as dark streaks mingle with the clear water, running thick and black then clearer and faster, into the gutters, the drains, and away.

The next morning, the sky was Mediterranean blue. The sun blazed down, scorching away the freshness of the storm. The air was hot and dry. Laura's fingers flew across the keys.

David was at the doorway. 'It's been on the radio,' he said. His voice had the lift of excitement. 'There's been another.'

'I know.'

She typed, the words spilling out of her fingers. She couldn't stop now, she mustn't stop. ...and the rainwater ran across the paving stones...

'Not the supermarket.' David wanted her attention. He had information to pass on, exciting news, and he couldn't wait to tell her. 'In the alleyway, Laura. They found her in the alleyway. Right behind our house! Last night.'

I know. But she couldn't say it.

Three a.m.

Something wakes her. She lies very still and listens. Silence. The wind whips the clouds across the moon. Light. Dark. Light. Dark. The curtains are pulled back and the trees in the garden make caves of shadow. They rock and sway. The branches of the cotoneaster scrape across the window. Tap. Tap. Tap. The alleyway is full of night.

David had been out all day, came back to find Laura at her desk, the dishes unwashed, the fridge empty.

He looked at the screen. 'Nothing. You've done nothing. Sitting there all day. I can't do it all.'

Sorry. I'm sorry. But she couldn't say it. Her eyes moved towards the window, where the buddleia flowers drooped over the high fence. A sudden breeze made them lift their heads. A piece of tape, yellow and black, danced through the air and wrapped itself round the stems, then hung still.

All day. She'd heard them there all day, behind the garden, in the alley.

Later, David relented. 'I've made you a sandwich.'

She couldn't choke it down.

'There's no pleasing you!'

She flinched as his hand brushed against hers.

His eyes were cold. 'Out. I'm going out. If you want to know.'

She couldn't worry about that now, couldn't let it distract her. Nothing else mattered now. She had to get back to her desk, back to her screen.

In the distance, she heard the door slam.

Laura sat in her study. The rain had started falling hours ago, and David had not come back. She read the words that filled the screen. She scrolled down, read. Her fingers tap tapped on the desk. She looked through her window. Now, it was dark outside, the back garden, and the fence, and the alleyway all in shadow, empty now and silent.

She went out into the corridor and opened the hall cupboard. The corridor was painted white, the walls satin, the doors gloss. The floor was polished. The light reflected into her eyes.

She opened the cupboard. She drummed her fingers, tap, tap against the door. She took off her slippers and put on a pair of black shoes, strappy, with very high heels. She had to fiddle with the fastenings for a few minutes. She stood up, tall and straight. She put on her coat, a mac, light and summery. It would be no protection against the rain. She threw a scarf, a summer scarf, thin and gauzy, round her neck. Then she walked to the door. Her heels tap, tap, tapped on the lino.

The street is long and straight, with pools of light under the streetlamps, light that glints off the water as it runs down the gutters. And between the lights, only shadows. The rain drips off the trees. Dark and then light. Dark and then light.

I can't find you any more!

I can't find you any more!

She walks on. She knows he will come. He has to.

Her feet tap tap on the pavement, moving quickly from light to light. And then she hears it. The sound of soft footsteps behind her, moving fast, moving closer.

Something glints in the darkness. Something blows in the wind, gauze and butterflies and flowers.

David gets home late. As he comes through the gate, he sees a curtain twitch in the house next door. He hesitates, then walks up the path. His own front door is open. He can hear it banging as the wind blows. He catches it before it can swing shut again, stands for a moment, listening. He looks at the window where the curtain moved. 'Laura?' he calls, and again, more loudly. 'Laura?' Then he closes the door quietly behind him.

The house is silent.

He goes to Laura's study. The screen flickers, the flowers and butterflies locked in their perpetual dance. He banishes them with a touch, and looks at the screen, looks at what Laura was writing, looks at the words that scroll down the screen.

The street was long and straight, with pools of light under the streetlamps, light that glinted off the water as it ran down the gutters. And between the lights, only shadows. The rain dripped off the trees. Dark and then light. Dark and then light.

I can't find you any more!

And then, over and over: No, no, no, no... down the screen. Down and down, no, no way, no way, no way. No..w no..w now now now.

He reaches out and presses a key. The writing jumps, fades, is gone.

The black screen faces him.

He smiles.

David Swann

has had five successes at the Bridport Prize, including three stories that are featured in his debut collection,

'The Last Days of Johnny North'
(Elastic Press, 2006)

His book, 'The Privilege of Rain' (Waterloo Press, 2010), was shortlisted for the 2011 Ted Hughes Award, and features reflections upon his work as writer-in-residence in a prison.

In 2013, David gained his second success in the National Poetry Competition and served as a judge for the Bridport Prize Flash Fiction Competition.

He divides his time between Brighton and Hove, where he is hard at work on a trilogy of novels and a book of micro-fiction.

He agrees with the German philosopher Anke Mittelberg that 'life is always worth living while there is a new type of cheese to discover.'

A former newspaper reporter, David is now a Senior Lecturer in English & Creative Writing at the University of Chichester.

Cock of The Block

I'm the third hardest lad on the top half of the left-hand side of our block. I used to be the eighth hardest until I gobbed Peter Pilkington, who was the third hardest, and so then I jumped up five places, which is why nobody messes with me now.

Unless you count Carl Smith. He's a bit of a stickler. Coming back from the pressed meat shop, I had to have a really long conversation with him about what he called The Correct Order. He wouldn't let it lie. The thing is, Bobby, he frowned – you can't be the third hardest because you're not as hard as Simon Clark.

Simon Clark? I said. Simon Clark is fourth cock, that's what he is. He can't even make proper gun noises!

What's that got to do with it? said Carl. He had biscuit crumbs on his lips again. And he smelled of gas. Plus, there was this funny look in his eye, like Lee Van Cleef in a Spaghetti western, right narrow and bright, as if he were facing me down a gun-barrel.

This is how Simon Clark makes gun noises, I said: phhh. phhhhh.

At least he can throw properly, said Carl. He mimed the way I was supposed to throw. He put his skinny arm out and pretended to chuck stones. It looked bad, right amateurish.

You want to watch it, you do, I said. I'm third cock of the...

Carl was throwing as if his arm had been broken in a terrible accident.

... of the... of...

Funny kind of third cock who can't beat up the fourth cock, said Carl, wandering off, still doing the mad thing with his arms.

I watched him disappear down our street. It occurred to me that Robin Walton wouldn't have stood for this. Robin Walton would have followed after Carl and stuck the nut on him.

Robin Walton was the cock of the block. Not just the top half of the left-hand side. I mean, the whole block. And he didn't even have to batter anybody to prove it.

But we're not talking about Robin Walton now. Got that straight? OK?

After Carl had gone, I was at a bit of a loose end. Mum & Dad had gone on nights at the wire factory again, so the only option was Gran's, and I thought I'd wait before putting myself through that. So I decided to count the number of weeds that were growing in the cracks between our pavements. It was quite difficult because some of the weeds were moss, which is like a weed that joins on, so I had to cheat, which is OK when no-one's watching. You can cheat if there's nobody else there. That's the rule.

There are all sorts of rules you have to stick to, even for cheating.

Course, they never leave you in peace. Up pops Derek Sardison, and he asks what I'm doing.

Who wants to know?

He looked down the street, as if at a loss. He's a pain in the neck, is Derek. Recently while I was walking up the street with him, he asked: Is it just me or is this hill getting steeper? That's why we call him the Young Aged Pensioner. On account of how weary he is.

Only, said Derek, only it looks like you were skenning at some sphagnum, Bobby.

So what if I was skenning at some sphagnum?

I was just saying, like. About that sphagnum, the way you were staring at it.

This sphagnum is none of your business, Derek. And, anyway, how come we've started saying sphagnum all the time? Nobody was saying sphagnum until you turned up.

I turned sideways so that Derek was out of sight. Out of my life, right.

Hmmm, said Derek, I can see now why you're acting the way you are.

Acting like what? I said.

It's probably because of that male pattern baldness you're suffering from...

I pretended not to take him on. I just let him stand there, staring at the side of my head. It's unusual for it to affect someone so young, isn't it, he said. Unusual in the case of a 12-year-old.

What is? I growled.

He went on staring at this point on the top of my head. He was nodding to himself in that way I hate, as if he's a wise person agreeing with an even wiser person. And yet he's not two wise people. He's Derek. He's one person, just about.

It'll probably all be gone by the time you're 30, he said. Whoosh – into the sink one morning. Blocking up the drains, and that. You'd better make the most if it while you still can, Bobby.

So what? I said. So what if it's gone by the time I'm 30? I won't care. I'll be ancient then. I'll be past caring.

Which was a phrase my Gran used whenever she predicted various agonising deaths. It was just a matter of time, she'd warned us. We're early die-ers, us lot. But you don't miss your life before you have it, so why should you miss it afterwards?

You'll be past caring when you're lying in your pit, Bobby!

Whoosh, I said to myself. Whoosh, bad memory.

Derek was skenning at me like he knew I was having a Mental Episode, muttering to myself. And I couldn't help it, but, even though I knew it would make me look soft, I touched my head with my fingers, just to check if it was true about the male pattern baldness.

I'll tell you what it is, I said to Derek, you ought to be more civil, you, Derek. (Another phrase I got from Gran. She had all sorts of phrases, did Gran. Whenever she stood up, she patted her sides and said, Kidneys, you're coming with me.)

Touchy, said Derek. It's not my fault if you're going bald.

I could have you any time I want, I warned Derek. You're not even included in the count. You aren't 40th cock of the left hand side. Or 80th. Or a millionth. You're not even bottom. You're just not included, Derek.

So put that in your pipe and smoke it!

Except – the next day, the lads up the spare-land had started going on about it too.

What's this about you being a slaphead? they asked. How come all your hair's falling out, Bobby?

I told them to remember it was my ball and I could take it home any time I liked, but it didn't seem to fuss them. They started calling me Friar Tuck. It didn't matter what I did to stop them – I even let them feel my hair. Look, I said, not a single piece missing!

But Simon Clark claimed he could see the first signs. Edison's Swirl, he called it: a set of circles that formed at the crown and then fanned out. Classic.

I did a Lee Van Cleef on Simon Clark. I squidged up my eyes and tried to make a crack for the light to glimmer in. Because eyes are the light of the body. That's what Gran said. We can choose to shine our light or cast our shadow. That was another of her sayings.

A wave of heat went through me. Who did Simon Clark think he was, anyway? Didn't he know the Correct Order?

Are you starting? he said.

Are you?

If you're starting, he said, then I'm finishing.

Go on then, I said.

Do you want it?

Have you got it?

Who wants to know?

Who's asking?

It got a bit tiring in the end, asking all those questions and pushing each other. Plus, my eyes ached from glimmering. Probably a slight strain. You need to be careful with your eyes, they're quite delicate. And, anyway, Simon Clark was too soft to start anything, so I grabbed my ball and went home. On the way, I whistled because I was still third cock of the top half of the left hand side. And Simon Clark was miles back, way down the list.

But what happens next, Simon Clark gets hold of a bell from somewhere and he comes past our house, ringing it. And it isn't any old bell either, but some massive thing like you'd get in a Mexican church in the westerns.

Hear ye! Hear ye! he was shouting.

Dong, goes the bell. Dong. You couldn't call it ringing. Toll would be the word. He was really tolling that bell. You could still hear it after he'd gone, even when he was miles down the street, chanting: Hear ye! Hear ye!

How come Simon Clark keeps walking past my house with a bell? I asked Derek Sardison.

Because of how bald you are, said Derek. He's going round with it, spreading the news.

I looked at him. Who is? I said. Who's bald?

You are, said Derek.

If this is about Edison's Swirl, I said, then let me tell you: there's no such thing. Ask anyone.

I would if I had the time, said Derek, but I've got more important things to be doing.

We stood outside my house, listening to the distant tolling.

This is all your fault, I said to Derek. You were the one who started this.

That's right, said Derek — shoot the pigeon, why don't you!

Where the hell did he get that bell from? I said.

They reckon he nicked it.

Nicked it off who?

Derek sighed. A dinner lady, he said.

A dinner lady?

They reckon he just took it off her. And there was nothing at all she could do. Because he's quite hard, is Simon Clark.

Hard? He's about as hard as toffee!

Toffee is hard, said Derek.

Yes, but it breaks easy. You can just snap it over your knee.

Not that anybody would actually do that, said Derek. Actually break toffee over their knee.

That isn't the point, I said. The point is: what's that bell got to do with anything? Why does Simon Clark keep ringing a bell outside my house?

Search me, said Derek.

But there was no chance of that. He sometimes put marshmallows in his pocket and forgot about them. You'd take your life in your hands, searching Derek Sardison.

At home that night, I started to think about the bell and whether it was true that Simon Clark had stolen it off a dinner lady. The thing that bothered me was that it was the summer holidays – baking hot, almost 65 degrees – and we weren't at school, so how could he have stolen it? I wriggled in my bed, struggling to sleep. Then it occurred to me that Simon must have gone to a dinner lady's house. He must have broken in.

I went into my Gran's room and asked her. Gran, I said, where do dinner ladies live?

She blinked in the light. What time is it? What the heck are you doing, wandering about in the middle of the night, Bobby?

I couldn't sleep, I said. I was thinking about dinner ladies.

Which dinner ladies?

All of them, I said.

She sighed, and put her head on the pillow. You'll drive me to the far end one of these days, you will, Bobby. Go back to sleep, lad.

How can I sleep, Gran? It isn't as easy as it seems. Whenever I shut my eyes, I start thinking about dinner ladies.

Look, she said: I don't want to hear any more about this. The only dinner lady I know, she lives in them bungalows up Millshaw way.

Just as I suspected, I said, in a sort of detective voice.

She turned and looked at me. Listen to me, Bobby, you're not to be oining any dinner ladies.

I won't, I said. I've never oined any dinner ladies before, have I, Gran?

No, she said, but you had some daft ideas about traffic wardens that time, didn't you?

This interview is terminated, I told her, and she sighed like Derek, which is allowed because she was Ancient and it's hard work for old folk, especially on these gradients.

After I'd had a poke around up at the bungalows, I decided to end that line of enquiries. The problem was that everybody who lived round there looked like a dinner lady and there was no way of knowing who might be hiding a bell.

And even if they were hiding one, it looked like Simon Clark had already nicked it, so what would be the point?

That was when two fit girls came past, laughing at me. Ey, they said – there's that slaphead again!

The one with Edison's Swirl?

The one who's going right bald.

You want to watch it, you two, I said. It doesn't matter how fit you think you are. I'm third cock of this block!

But only the top half.

On the left hand side.

And you're not even that, anyway. Because Simon Clark is harder.

He is not, I said.

Then how come he's going round calling you Friar Tuck and ringing that bell?

I shrugged. Probably because he's got nowt better to do.

He'll batter you if he hears you say that.

I'll tell you summat about that Simon Clark, I said. He's boring and soft and he's ashamed of his Mum for being a dinner lady.

His Mum? The one who works in the chemist's, you mean?

Pah, I said. You fell for it. That chemist's is just a front.

The girls frowned. What's a front?

Something that isn't real. Something that's been invented to make the real thing look like it was invented.

They giggled nervously.

To think, I said: that someone should stoop so low as to steal a bell from their own mother! I said this in the voice I'd learned from my Gran. Quite angry and saddened. It's the voice she uses to talk about all the dog dirt there is on the streets these days.

That night my Gran stopped eating and stared at her fork. We were having my least favourite meal: sprouts and potatoes and gravy. Well, she was having it. I was just looking at it, waiting for it to turn into real food.

Some idiot's ringing a bell, she said. Can you hear it, Bobby? A really loud bell?

I went on staring at the sprouts. Except not really looking at them, just staring to one side, like an antelope that's having its neck bitten out by a lion in a documentary.

Dong.

Happen it's a dinner lady who's gone wrong, I grunted.

Gran thought about that while studying her fork. I once knew a dinner lady who had had a bad do with her nerves, she said. She ran off to Aberdeen.

Dong.

Or was it Stenhousemuir? said Gran.

I nodded vaguely.

Dong.

Some place with a funny name, anyway. Eee. My memory, lad.

Gran, I said: was Granddad bald? When he was young, I mean? Did he lose his hair when he was young?

Granddad? she smiled. Granddad never had a hair on his head in all the years I knew him. It passed down through the genes, see. His family curse.

I touched my head again, tried to act casual.

Aye, she said. He got it from his mother, I think.

His mother?

Your great-grandmother, that would be. They were all like that, the lasses on your grandad's side. Bald as coots, some of them.

A coot? What's a coot, Gran?

A bird, I think.

A bald bird?

Suppose so, she said. It's just a turn of phrase. Blimey, lad – the face on you. Honestly. And sighing, too. It isn't healthy to be sighing so much, a young lad like you!

I whacked the chair back and stood up. Sighing, I said. I wasn't sighing. It was you sighing. I never sigh. I hardly ever sigh.

Steady on.

I'm sick of people who sigh! I shouted.

And that was me, gone through the sliding door, which was rubbish because you couldn't even slam it, and then you were in the kitchen, a pointless room because it had no back door and you couldn't get out, so you were stuck, pretending that you'd meant to go in there anyway, probably to look for a spoon or something. And you were looking at the sliding door, which didn't even slide – it just, sort of, bunched up. And who the hell puts a bunchy door on the end of their living room? What do they think they're living in? A train?

Don't even think of sneaking any of that pudding, Gran warned from the living room. Not while there are all them sprouts on your plate.

That night, I realised there was only one thing for it. I had to get that bell off Simon Clark and give it back to the dinner lady or throw it in a lake.

After all, Simon Clark was the reason that everybody was calling me Friar Tuck and spreading rumours about the Correct Order.

So that was that then. I made up a detailed plan. It was to do with going round to Simon Clark's house and telling him to give me the bell or I'd gob him. There was a bit more to it than that, of course – a lot of classified details that I can't go into – but you get the gist.

Well, it was just the sort of house you'd expect. They'd painted the door mustard and there were those daft bubbles in the window so it looked like they had tits stuck to the front of their house.

How come you've got tits everywhere? I said when Simon came to the door.

He blinked a couple of times. Then he said: I've warned you, Friar Tuck. Do you like hospital food?

Probably better than your Mum's cooking. Anyway, who wants to know?

Are you talking to me or chewing a brick?

How'd you like to pick your teeth up with a broken arm?

You'll not be so chirpy when you have to suck your food through a straw.

I do that, anyway, with my Gran's cooking, so it won't bother me, I said.

That was when a familiar voice came floating down the corridor: Simon! Shut that flaming door!

Simon looked back down the passage of his home, a bit nervous. He rubbed his arm. The voice shouted louder: Simon! The door!

Then a shape appeared, tall and wide, filling the passageway. The shape was wearing a tee-shirt and boxer shorts. The boxer shorts had a snooker table design on the front, a triangle of red balls waiting to be potted.

It was Robin Walton, the cock of everywhere. He looked a bit grieved.

Sorry, said Simon. I was just dealing with something, Robin.

The tracing paper, said Robin. The draught from this door nearly ruined the tracing paper, Simon.

He was holding a pair of scissors, the girlie type – pinking shears, their blades all crinkly. He said to Simon: Look. Are we getting these trousers done, or what?

Simon Clark nodded. Yes, we are. That's right, Robin.

Simon turned back to me. Scram, slaphead, he said.

Who are you calling a slaphead, you bell-ender? I said.

Bell-enders were lads with funny-shaped doo-dahs. I thought it'd be a good thing to call him, given the way he'd been acting. Given his recent antics.

Look, he said – if this is about the bell-ringing – I'll tell you something about that bell: it's made my arm right sore, and I'm blaming you for that. I can barely move it to cut out the patterns.

More like because you've been donging your bell-end, I said.

Robin laughed suddenly, a nasty sort of laugh, like a hound on the trail of blood. Heh, he said. Heh heh. Simon's arm's right sore because he's been pulling the ropes in his belfry, he gasped. Isn't that right, Friar Tuck!

For a minute, I was a bit confused that Robin Walton was talking to me, what him being the hardest lad in at least Lancashire, so I just stared at him while he cackled, trying to work out what came next, what I was supposed to do.

After he should have stopped laughing, he carried on, until I was worried the joke would burst him open and something else might fall out, this weird thing that had been inside Robin Walton, working the controls.

I don't know what you're both on about, said Simon Clark. My arm aches because of Friar Tuck here. Because I've to ring a massive bell all the time.

But Robin was gasping for air, and coughing. He had to grope with his hands for the wall, like he was falling. Ey, he managed to say, finally. One of you's a slaphead and the other just slaps it about!

That did it. He fell onto his knees, gasping. Simon didn't move, nor did I. We watched Robin wipe his face with both hands, as if he were trying to pull off a mask.

I like your style, he gasped. That's quality, that is, Friar Tuck. You're a good laugh, you are. For a slaphead, anyway. At any rate, you're better company than this one. See the state of it. Face like a kicked arse.

Simon rubbed his sore arm. Look, he said: do you want those trousers altering, or not?

Ooo, said Robin. Get her.

He led Simon back up the corridor, into Simon's own house, and I followed them because I didn't know what else I was supposed to do, because Robin was the cock and only he knew the rules.

In the living room, they'd laid Robin's trousers against a massive length of tracing paper marked with various black lines.

Careful where you tread, Simon Clark grunted.

I hung back, watching him kneel over the design. Robin Walton stood above, scowling so hard I thought I could hear cracks opening in his head.

The left hem, he pointed.

I know, said Simon.

And straighter.

I'm doing it.

All the way down.

I need to concentrate, Robin.

But the edges – they're supposed to be drainpipes.

They will be drainpipes.

Flares are out now.

So you keep saying.

They won't shag a lad in flares. Isn't that right, Mr Tuck?

I pressed my trousers together, to make them look narrow. Yes, I said. Flares are for squares, Robin.

He liked that. He laughed so hard that he had to bend over, as if he'd left his breath on the floor. For squares, he said. Are you listening, Simon? Flares are for squares!

Simon gasped, impatiently. When you're done, he said, if it isn't too much bother, happen you'd pass me the shears, finally.

Robin did as he was told, studying the pattern carefully as he recovered his breathing. Meanwhile Simon Clark crawled around the carpet on his knees, crinkling the paper.

You missed a bit, said Robin.

Simon went back over the line.

Imagine the birds when they see these! Robin beamed. They'll go goggle-eyed, eh, Mr Tuck?

Yes, I said.

Yes! He roared. And that was that – he was off again. Gasping.

I watched Simon cut around the outline with the scissors. Who taught you how to do that? I asked him.

This? Who do you think?

His Mum doesn't just give him blow-jobs, you know, spluttered Robin.

Simon lifted the trousers off the carpet. I'll need to take these upstairs to the sewing machine, he said.

Make it snappy then, said Robin. If I have to sit here any longer in my undies, this one might get ideas in his head. Eh, Mr Tuck!

Yes, I said.

Yes! he roared.

I stood at the back of the living room, listening to Simon's slow feet on the stairs. When he reached the landing, there was silence for a moment, then a thump, as if he'd dropped a box or kicked something. After that, there was a click and then the sound of the sewing machine.

Good luck, that, his Mum being a professional mender, said Robin.

I scratched my head. Isn't she a dinner lady? Or a chemist?

Robin slathered himself over the settee. He grabbed the remote control and gave it a click. He could click it louder than other people.

Do you like comedies? he said.

Upstairs, Simon's feet were pumping the treadle.

Robin spread his legs as wide as they'd go. His thighs were as thick as a farmer's. Hairy, too. I imagined them bulging out of the drainpipes that Simon was making for him.

This one's good, he said, pointing the remote at the TV. I like it, this one. It's a good laugh, is this. There's this lodger who's come to stay. And the married couple can't get rid of him. It's right good. They don't have any proper furniture. They sit in deckchairs in their living room. Have you seen it?

No, I said, staring at his thighs. I've never seen it.

Well, you should, said Robin. You haven't lived unless you've seen a comedy like this.

I leaned against the back wall, listening to Simon working on Robin's trousers upstairs. The noise of the machine was nearly loud enough to drown out the telly, but it was no match for Robin's laughs. He yelped like a gibbon through the whole programme, even during the adverts, including the ones for dogmeat that weren't funny, just the bits where women held up tins and said dogmeat was brilliant.

It cracks me up, that one, he said. It's good, isn't it? What a laugh, eh!

Yes, I said.

His face hardened, just for a second. Then he turned back to the telly and started laughing again. You're alright, you are, he said. You've got a sense of humour. Not like some I could mention.

When I left, he was still lying with his massive legs wide apart, stroking the remote control and barking out laughs. It was his underpants that made me hate him, I think. The stupid snooker balls on them.

The sound of Simon's sewing machine followed me out up the street, all the way to the top half of the street. I looked back down the block before going in to see my Gran. I was sure I could still hear Robin laughing. It wasn't a sound with any fun in it. It sounded like he was trying to force a flag into a mountain top.

When I got in, Gran was lying on the couch, having a bit of a spell before the soaps came on.

She was a bit off, she said. Her skin was aching.

What, all of it? I asked.

All of the top half, she said. And a fair bit of the bottom half. It's the weather, lad. This flaming heat. Where have you been, anyway? You didn't go oining any dinner ladies, did you?

Phhh, I said, disgusted. What do you think I am, Gran? A death-squad, or something?

She gave me a funny look.

Gran, I said, if Mum & Dad earn a bit more on the night-shift, happen I'll get extra pocket money, do you think?

Mmmm, she said.

So I was thinking – if I saved up for the material, would you make me some trousers?

She was tending to her aching skin, and just grunted, a bit off-hand.

Only – I need some drainpipes, I said. It's important I get some drainpipes.

Drainpipes, is it? said Gran. What's wrong with the trousers you're wearing?

Flares? I said. Flares are for squares, Gran.

Aye well, she said, I wouldn't know anything about that, Bobby. We're still wearing sack-cloth down this end.

I wouldn't get any sense of out her in a mood like that, I could see clear enough. Instead, I just sat there and watched her put the telly on. It was a comedy and Gran scowled at the screen like she was chewing glass.

They're all dead, you know, she said, after a while.

Who are, Gran?

The audience. They taped them years ago, and it's always the same people laughing.

On every programme?

As far as I know, lad. Makes you think, doesn't it?

Yes, I said.

But it didn't, because I wasn't even watching. While Gran scowled at the screen, I just went on studying my thighs.

Maybe I didn't need a new pair of trousers. Maybe I just needed a few alterations.

In the background, I could hear hundreds of people laughing. They sounded like Robin Walton. They sounded dead.

I hated his guts, and he was everything I wanted to be. Work that one out, if you're so flaming clever!

I can't see why you're laughing, said Gran, shaking her head. It isn't even funny, lad.

No, I said. You're right, Gran. It isn't even funny.

She watched the comedy right through without a single reaction, and then the soaps came on. During the soaps, she mainly watched the curtains and the wallpaper. Hardly any of the things in the background suited the things in the foreground, all the settees and the cushions, and that. It was like they'd fished the whole lot out of a skip.

You'd think they'd get it right, the money they spend, wouldn't you, lad?

You would, Gran. Yes.

And who's that supposed to be, anyway? Is he the bloke who did the murder?

Which murder?

The murder last week.

I didn't watch it last week, Gran. I was out then.

It was true, too. I'd been out gobbing Peter Pilkington while Gran was watching last week's episode. That's how I came to be the third cock of the top half of the left-hand side of our block.

That was yonks ago now, though. Ancient history. I'd got bigger fish to fry these days. I was working on my thighs now.

I was thinking about my new trousers.

Henry Shukman

is a prize-winning poet and novelist whose works have been Book of the Year in the *Guardian* and *Times* of London, Editor's Choice in the *New York Times*, and have won the Arts Council England Award. Originally from Britain, he lives with his wife and two sons in Santa Fe, New Mexico, where he is the resident teacher at Mountain Cloud Zen Center. He is a Zen teacher in the Sanbo Zen lineage of Kamakura, Japan.

The Venice Faxes

It is three months now since we lost Sally Splinter. She had been travelling on assignment for our 'Venice in Peril' Committee, of which she was an enthusiastic member, when she met her tragic end.

The following will shed no light on her unexpected death, but will at least reassure all that Sally's last hours were happy. Since the latest 'facsimile' technology generates a full set of correspondence for both parties, sent and received, we have assembled in this little pamphlet Sally's exchanges from Venice verbatim, even where some of us may not appear in the most flattering light.

No doubt we will all be inspired to make a reality her dream of Saving Santa Monica. Don't miss the October Ball! (Contact the Porters Lodge for tickets @ £75 each.)

Dame Cynthia Templeton,
Warden,
Senior Common Room,
Jesus College,
Cambridge.

FAO: Dame Cynthia Templeton.
From: Sally Splinter, La Residenza, Venezia.
9 May, 1981, 2.38 P.M.

Dear Cynthia,

Receive this in the personal line, not the official. Don't think I've been neglecting my mission, however; report to follow.

Venice is surpassing itself. I always forget, don't you? The first vaporetto trip and the magic reawakens as if it has been hidden inside one all along, waiting for the first kiss of Venetian light.

To the point: I think I just may have found us a new project. I know I know, that's not what I'm supposed to be doing, but hear me out. I've been to the Scuola di San Rocco Cellars already, I've done everything I should have, I'm not being slack. But darling, I have found us a gem, an ecstasy of a church, a place you start loving before you even see it. You feel it from around the corner.

Drifting my way back from the Scuola, I stopped in at a trattoria for mezzogiorno (the most wonderful prosecco – I'm a complete convert) and all through lunch I had this strange extra feeling. Afterwards, I sort of glided round the corner, as if I knew what I was going to see, and came face to face with the most beautiful, and crumbling, facade. Tail-end Romanesque, just the right time, with a heavenly weave of white and green marble, and brickwork of that warm burgundy only the Venetians knew how to bake.

It has its own little courtyard in front (flagstones) and sits on its own little canal near the Ghetto.

Let me know ASAP if I may pursue. Holding breath, crossing fingers,
Sally

To: Sally Splinter, c/o La Residenza, Venezia.
From: Cynthia Templeton, Jesus College
Monday 9th May, 5.11 P.M.

Page 1 of 1

Yes, dear, very interesting, but what's it called? And what does 'FAO' mean?
Best,
Cynthia

FAO: Cynthia
From: Sally
May 9, 1981, 6.17 P.M.

Page 1 of 3

Dear Cynthia: *Santa Monica Dell'Orto.* Monica of the Orchard.

(FAO, FYI, means ATTN. Where have you been mouldering?)

First things first. Even on the boat taxi from the airport, shared with a German couple (Berliners, black hair, black clothes, black bags) I saw something miraculous. There we are, racing across the muddy brown lagoon, a row of barber's poles guiding us, when all of a sudden a buoy bobs up from the waves ahead. It sinks and rises again, and just as we approach it, a human figure emerges from the waters, standing up right out there in the middle of the lagoon. The buoy is his head. Not only is he naked, but golden. Bright gold. Is it the mud in sunshine? His wet tan? The Venetian light? I say 'his' but I can't really see if it's man or woman, with the sunlight blazing on the water. He sank back into the waves as we passed and when I looked back he was gone. It was so almost-absurd, so dreamy. So Venetian. It makes one want to laugh, or cry.

No sooner have I dumped my bags at La Residenza (another story) than I trundle off to Signor Pranzo at the UNICEF office. What an office. It made me wonder: am I the right person to represent us? Why not Lady Oliver, or you, Dame Cynthia? Why lowly me, crawling out of the History Department?

Page 2 of 3

Up princely stairs, down an immense corridor, into a vestibule the size of our chapel lined with silk from the Pucci mills – all original eighteenth c. A chandelier the size of a car, glass knives tinkling in the breeze. Creaky wooden floors, antique desks, lots of clutter, papers everywhere, and huge. Huge room, huge windows. You can make as much mess as you like in an office like that. The space eats it up for you.

Signor Pranzo wears slacks, loafers, a blue shirt open at collar. We went over everything properly and bureaucratically (all of which will appear in report – to come), then he gave me, for interest's sake, a list of every building in Venice currently needing 'estabilizazzione', as they euphemistically call it. They mean saving.

It's after lunch, strolling along the Canale di San Martino, aglow with prosecco, that I find her. I knew exactly where to go, and there she was. I felt like I could have walked on water.

What a pitiful state she's in. Half the marble fallen from the facade and lying on the paving in fragments. You can see the brown moisture half way up the walls. Disastrous. And all crumbling and disastrous-looking inside too. But at once you know it's a dream of a church. Small and perfect. And when I drifted into the Lady Chapel at the back I realized I had arrived at the source of what had come over me.

Sitting in one corner was a great lump of marble, an unfinished statue of Santa Monica, the limbs and hands and face still in the act of being born. It was found it in an orchard

in 1370 and the Venetians decided it was miraculous and built the church for it. Who else on earth would do that?

I'm skeptical as the next, but that madonna half-hewn from a block by an anonymous medieval sculptor sat bathed in its own light. It glowed, it shone, it hovered. Her face bends low over her legs. She's sort of hunched up, head tipped to one side. She has a beautiful face, even if it's only in rough, with a sort of smile, not exactly a smile. She looked at me. Stopped me in my tracks. A human face. A wonderful mother, something like that, the mother none of us ever had (except your boys) and when you see her you feel you've known her all your life.

Basta. Enough incoherence. Tomorrow Signor Pranzo and I talk to the padre.

Sally.

To: Sally
From: Cynthia
10 May, 1981, 8.36 A.M.

Page 1 of 1

Darling,

You are our representative over there. You're supposed to be sending back reports. Letters are decidedly welcome of course, but I can't very well hand them to the Committee. And Venice is full of heavenly churches in need of help. But still... it does sound exciting. We'll have some convincing to do, so 'Fax' back AT ONCE with more.

Love, Cynthia.

P.S. As for my going to Venice instead of you, don't be absurd. You are just the person. By the way, I have given your fax number to your student Marion Gornick. She's in rather a state.

P.P.S. And what might 'FYI' mean, Daughter of Tomorrow?

P.P.P.S. Aren't these machines fun? One feels terribly important.

FAO: Sally
From: Cynthia Templeton. S.C.R. Jesus College.
10 May, 1981, 12.02P.M.

Page 1 of 1

Well? I've been waiting all morning...

FAO: Cynthia
From: Sally.
10 May, 1981, 1.33 P.M.

Page 1 of 2

Cynthia:
I always thought I was a morning person, but I'm not, I'm a lunch person. Despite last night's Campari(s) I feel deliciously alert just now.

Sorry last was so long. This threatens to be as bad. Today has been quite a day.

I saw Pranzo at the UNICEF office first thing. There's a complication. Santa Monica isn't even on his list. He couldn't say why, she just slipped through. Some do. 'Everything's ad hoc,' he said. 'Half our task is simply to address that.' They're in process, he says (bureaucrats talk like psychologists these days – does everyone?). It's a miracle I found her.

Everyone is terribly understanding and terribly scientific. Everyone? There are three girls in the office, and a Signor Fratelli from the Venice City Council who has to take every project to his Councillors. He doesn't think there's likely to be any objection to helping Santa Monica. He's going to come up with me to have a 'look about.'

(Just ordered spag vongole and a glass of Trentino-Baggio. Mmm.)

Down to business. Fratelli, of the City Council: a roly-poly man, frightfully Italian, wears a vest under his shirt, and one of those strimmered beards. The dear has been invaluable. He got the plans for the church from the Officina delle Labori della Citta – the O.L.C., don't forget that, they're important. Apparently the church is sinking. So what's new? But water is also rising up the stonework. Capillary action, I think (vague memory from O-level Chemistry). But if they slice through the masonry and insert a copper sheet, and if all the masonry above is soaked in acid, then... maybe. And there's a Bellini. A raggedy Pieta, but a Bellini none the less. It'll need to be taken to the Ospedale di Santa Croce, a sort of hospital for pictures.

Aha. My vongole have arrived. Till later,

S.

Almost forgot: For Your Information.

FAO: Marion Gornick.
From: Sally Splinter.
10 May, 1981, 4.15 P.M.

Page 1 of 1

Sweetheart, Marion,

If-oh-oh-only you were here... You would feel so much better, you would understand why this life is for you (though I appreciate your worries). Venice is the godmother of us downhill tweedies – I don't mean you, of course. It was always a city for visitors with souls unencumbered by the day-to-day of procreation – Venice's Vestals, the ones with space in our hearts, our ears not drowned by infants' cries.

Am I laying it on a bit thick? How are you? Are things any clearer? I hated to leave you in such a state, with so much happening and so much to decide. For what it's worth, I'm more convinced than ever of what I've said all along. Not only are you far too good to hide in a bungalow on the fringes of Cleveland, wherever that is, but this is the life for you. You are made for it as no one I've known before. You can't imagine the riches awaiting you.

Fax me here. Aren't these instant letters fun? Miss you, miss you,

Sally.

FAO: Sally
From: Cynthia Templeton. S.C.R. Jesus College
10 May, 1981, 6.06 P.M.

Page 1 of 1

Sally? Well? Are you there? It's Tuesday night and I'm sitting here next to this contraption waiting for it to warble and chatter, and give me news of you.

I have news for you, actually. Your student Marion came to see me again. She's terribly nice, terribly unhappy. I think you should talk to her asap. She was in an almighty panic about her thesis binding or some such. You can 'fax' her here and I won't read. Promise. Scout's.

Love, Cynthia.

Attn: Sally Splinter.
From: Marion Gornick, Jesus College Library.
10 May, 1981, 6.15 P.M.

Page 1 of 1

Dearest Sally,

I'm so sorry to bother you when you have so much on your plate and the last thing you want to think about is little old me stuck in the rain (constant since you left), but I'm just so churned up at the moment, I don't know what to do. Tom has been calling all the time. He says the prospect of leaving has made him realize that he can't go without me etc. etc. What do I do? Do I want to become little wifey in Ohio?

I feel awful talking about all this when you're busy doing Important Things. I got your fax number from Dame Templeton. I hope you don't mind. (I told her it was about my thesis.)

And actually I'm worried about that too. The binder needs to know what binding I want. There's about sixty different kinds and he's being so nasty and sort of: well what can I do about it ma'am? I wish he wouldn't call me ma'am.

Help. All love, Marion.

P.S. Just got your message. Heaven. I can't tell you how much better I felt the instant I walked into the Lodge and saw the fax scroll filling up my pigeon-hole. Such a strange time, all these opportunities at once. Tom and I had lunch today and of course it was nice, not having seen each other in a while. And no I didn't, in case you're wondering. We had a drink in the Granta (I ordered Campari, just for you), then said goodbye and that I would continue to think. Very firm and simple. But shaking inside. Are you sure no one can read this? I'm terrified the machine has a memory and will spew it all out.

M.

FAO: Cynthia
From: Sally.
10 May, 1981, 7.03 P.M.

Page 1 of 1

Dear Cynthia, Didn't you get my message of earlier? Sending again. And thanks re. Marion. Just heard from her.

S.

FAO: Sally.
From: Cynthia.
11 May, 1981, 1.12P.M.

Page 1 of 1

Darling,

Found both copies of your last – ta. I've had a word with a couple of the Committee members who reminded me that the point of the San Rocco Cellars is that we know precisely what is involved, what it will cost and what our 'input' will achieve. Do you really think you can pull off something new in so little time? You haven't given us much to go on. Yes it's pretty, yes it needs work, but...

More, please, more... Cynthia.

FAO: Marion Gornick.
From: Sally.
11 May, 1981, 6.45 P.M.

Page 1 of 1

Dearest Marion,

You know more about these new-fangled machines than I do but I can't imagine they would waste their time regurgitating my verbiage. Apparently our messages crossed.

Re. Campari: I'm having one now just for you, sitting on my balcony overlooking an adorable piazza. Boys bouncing a football, a lovely plain church, a couple of almond trees, sun setting, pen in hand.

I've found us the most wonderful church. You must come and see it. Somebody said that a city comes alive when you love someone in it, and they were right. I can't tell you how I feel, knowing Santa Monica is just there, a mile away over the rooftops. The only thing missing is you.

Now listen, dear. Don't do anything. Let it all drop for a day or two. You have nothing to worry about, although it doesn't look that way to you. You're a brilliant woman with a wonderful career ahead of her. If you throw it away in order to play wife on some ghastly mid-western campus you'll never forgive yourself. I've seen it time and again, there's nothing worse than the life of a campus wife. It's like being an army wife only – only worse. Hold your ground. And re. your thesis: go to the man in Botolph Lane, he's done a million theses, and tell him I personally gave strict instructions that he is to do the usual. He'll know what I mean.

Of course Tom would be calling just when he's about to leave. He's terrified. But what didn't work once won't work again. Don't worry, that's the main thing. If you don't worry you can see the wood for the trees. And your Fellowship is a foregone thing, as you ought to know. It's just a matter of paperwork.

Remember you're my little star. No setting just yet.

No one speaks a word of English here. You can write what you like. Just trust and have faith. You're the best.

Here's looking at you, kid

(Campari-clink).

FAO: Cynthia.
From: Sally.
11 May, 1981, 7.16 P.M.

Page 1 of 1

Cynthia:

Right. Down to business. Fratelli took me back to the church. He knew the padre, who lives a few steps away, sunk deep in an armchair from which he entertained us with porto bianco – a bit rich for ten in the morning. Of the church he kept repeating, 'E grande cosa, e grande cosa.' He still conducts services among the rubble. I liked him. Flabby cheeks, flabby throat spilling over his collar, and all trembly with drink, but sort of soft and reassuring. One would feel safe going to confession with him. He was a ruin like his church.

Fratelli was jovial, boisterous, deferential, and somewhere in the course of their conversation, which I only half managed to follow because the priest had a terrible habit of mumbling into his chest, Fratelli apparently succeeded in gaining the man's approval for restoration work. So he said, anyway, once we were outside. So it looks like it's a 'go.'

Keep you posted, S.

To: Sally.
From: Marion.
12 May, 1981, 8.30 A.M.

Page 1 of 1

Dearest Sally,
What's the use of trusting and having faith if you don't do something? Staying here when I could go there, etc., etc. – it feels like turning my back on life.

Awake all last night. If only you were here.
Marion.

FAO: Sally.
From: Cynthia.
12 May, 1981, 5.13 P.M.

Page 1 of 1

Sally,
You've got me on tenterhooks. Are we going to have to throw another ball? Another dinner? How much? Have we got enough? What's the 'bottom line'?

C.

To: Marion.
From: Sally.
12 May, 5.45 P.M.

Page 1 of 1

Darling Marion,

Just got back. Sorry to keep you waiting. How can embracing your talents and putting them to their best use be to turn your back on life? Relax. Wait. At least until I get back.

Kisses, Sally.

FAO: Cynthia.
From: Sally.
May 12th, 5.51 P.M.

Page 1 of 1

Cynthia,

How much? I don't know yet. Fratelli is working night and day to sort things out. Santa Monica will need the same water tanks for the *acque alte* as San Rocco. Can we do another fundraiser? Would it be too awful to change projects? So many people are pouring money into San Rocco as it is, and if we're really honest, were we ever terribly excited about saving some dreary cellars and a humdrum crucifixion cycle by unknown assistants? Wouldn't it be divine to have our own project, rather than just taking up the slack in some Minnesota chapter's? The Jesus Venice Project – Saving Santa Monica!

You should see the signor here in the hotel. He emerges from behind his enormous cluttered desk frowning, conjuring endless scrolls of thin, shiny paper – your faxes. Victorian circus-man sideburns, the ubiquitous pasta belly. Pasta bellies are more attractive than beer bellies. Maybe I'll move here and grow one.

Marion's fragile. Look after her. At least — not too well, you understand. She's fiercely bright, and really there's nothing else she could happily do than be a don, but she's going through a tricky phase. I told her last week we'd have her, junior fellow and so on. Be nice.

Hugs, Sally.

ATTN: SALLY SPLINTER, Ph.D.,
From: The Bursar, Jesus College, Cambridge
13 May, 1981, 9.39 A.M.

Page 1 of 1

Dear Miss Splinter,

Lady Templeton has kindly brought me up to date as regards your progress in Venice.

I feel I should remind you that at the Governing Body Meeting of April 11th, the Senior Fellows agreed to allocate a part of this year's Budget Surplus Fund towards a Charitable Project. As I believe you are aware, these funds amount to a little over £94,000, and I understand that a suitable project has already been earmarked for them in Venice. I must stress that I see no likelihood of further funds becoming available this fiscal year.

If in fact it turns out there are other projects the Save Venice Committee might like to help sponsor, there may be further opportunities in future fiscal years.

FAO: Cynthia
From: Sally
13 May, 1981, 10.15 A.M.

Page 1 of 1

Cynthia,

The beastly bursar has sent me a letter. Blah blah blah. He called you 'Lady.'

Fratelli and the O.L.C. are working on a 'Plan of Priorities' for Santa Monica. The Bellini, for example, isn't urgent. Most urgent are floor and walls. Then roof, apparently. Here the greatest danger is from below. Fratelli says a conservative estimate of the initial costs for 'stabilizing' her might be around £250,000. I know it's a lot but we can do it bit by bit. He says he can break it down for me and I'll affix his report to mine. We could raise the funds in stages, ball by ball, raffle by raffle.

Report should be ready soon.

Love,

S

FAO: Sally.
From: Cynthia.
13 May, 1981, 10.30 A.M.

Page 1 of 1

Darling,

I'm sure it's a beautiful church but of course we can't ask the governing body to stretch to £250,000. Don't be absurd. And you can't raise quarter of a million with raffles. Go to Harry's Bar, have a Bellini or three, relax.

Cynthia.

FAO: Cynthia
From: Sally
13 May, 1981, 7.30P.M.

Page 1 of 2

Darling Cynthia,

Something wonderful has happened. You're going to think I'm mad. I think I'm mad, except if I am I want to be.

She moved. She lifted her head and smiled at me. I have never seen such a smile.

Do you remember Bill Wright, the travel writer who spent a term at the college? He once told me a story about swimming with whales off Patagonia. The moment he slipped into the water he felt an all-pervasive love envelope him. He was aware of a presence passing beneath him like a bus, and a moment later the giant whale surfaced, and a gentle eye looked at him. He had never felt so much love as in that gaze.

I have felt the same thing. I was sitting all alone in the Lady Chapel of Santa Monica. Occasionally there's a dear old man who carries a broom around the church never quite bringing himself to actually make contact with the floor, but he was nowhere to be seen. Mid morning, very quiet. The whispered scuffle of a pigeon alighting outside. The blurry shadow of a tree brushing back and forth across a dusty window. We're sitting there, just the two of us, just me and Santa Monica in stone, and I'm experiencing a curious peace, almost like a déja vu, when gently it dawns on me that she is looking at me.

I don't know how to explain. I keep trying phrases and none fits. First of all, the stone is a lovely pale marble. Second, there's something mystifying about those half-carved features. Third, the stone seems to attract light. The rest of the room could be in gloom but the statue would still be bathed in a dreamy desert light. As I looked up she raised her head – just

113

a little, but unmistakably – and smiled at me. A smile that didn't so much register in my eyes as my chest. As if she shone within me. I blinked and coughed and it made no difference, she was still smiling at me.

I never felt anything like it. A fullness in my heart as if a flame has been lit. What is the flame? What is its fuel? Love and love. Love for what? For nothing, for everything. Now, hours later, she still comes with me everywhere. Who is she? Whoever she is, I am hers, always have been and always will be. Everything but everything makes sense. I know now that our work, I mean our academic work, is valuable, and I also know it's not. But it has a place, it belongs in a scheme. Isn't that wonderful? S.

FAO: Sally
From: Cynthia
13 May, 1981, 8.20 P.M.

Stendhal Syndrome. Obviously. Oh lucky lucky you. I'm devilishly jealous.

This is all marvellous, darling, but where is our report!? The Bursar is getting uneasy. You've been there five days, all these faxes coming in, and no report on his desk. Where is it? You must sit down and write to him, to us. You are our deputy.

Are you sure you're quite well? Ought you to look in on the hotel doctor?

Ciao, Cynthia.

To: Sally Splinter
From: Marion Gornick
13 May, 1981, 4.15 P.M.

Page 1 of 1

Dearest Sally,

Just had dinner with Tom. He keeps telling me America is the place to be, I'll get a job over there, it's the future of civilization, a new life waiting for us. I listen to him and see his hopefulness and such a promising look in his eyes and I think he's right, why turn my back on the future? How can I possibly disappoint this man? But then I come home and before I even open the door I realize I'm terrified of going, and that the prospect of staying here with such a good job (you're so kind to have set it up) is something I couldn't contemplate rejecting. What shall I do?

All love, Marion.

FAO: Cynthia
From: Sally
14 May, 1981, 9.43P.M.

Page 1 of 1

C: I went to see the priest again. I rapped on his door and waited five minutes then it opened a crack and he looked me up and down, just like in the movies. We sat in silence, both of us deeply comfortable. I felt so at home. Then I told him, I just came right out with it: she smiled at me, I said. He nodded and smiled too, and I knew he understood. She is divine. It's for real. There are more things in heaven and earth...

The Padre says every day he expects to find that the statue has dropped clean through the paving and sunk without trace in the swamp beneath the city.

About the bursar. At first I thought: how can the man be so unimaginative and dull? Fly him out here! Let him see for himself. If we're going to have a Jesus Venice Project then why do it by halves? But then I thought of Monica and realized even the Bursar is forgiven. She forgives everyone. And she needs no vessel. Churches and cities may crumble but she will live on. She is not of stone, though she occupies it for now.

Loving wishes, S.

P.S. Actually I did go to the doctor after having two dizzy spells yesterday. He's given me the all-clear. Says I should rest. Venice make peoples sick because they walk and walk, breathing the bad airs and won't take the boat.

FAO: Marion
From: Sally
15 May, 1981, 8.23P.M.

Page 1 of 2

Saturday morning. The first day of life!

Dearest Marion,

You can't turn your back on the future, my sweet. It's simply impossible. It doesn't matter where you go or what you do, it doesn't even matter if you are dead or alive, you can't escape the divine scheme which holds us all in its love. You have to find whatever will bring you to that love in yourself.

I never told you this but Venice is a special place for me for a reason. The first time I came I thought I was going to marry. I came with him, George. We had recently decided. I had done a year of my Ph.D., he was working outside Ely (there used to be an electronics plant there, part of Marconi) and they were going to send him to Wales as a manager in a new plant. Of course I was planning to go with him. That was 1956. We came to Venice for a weekend, an extravagance the like of which we'd never approached before, a celebration of his new job and our engagement. I just wasn't even in the picture, really, his picture or my own. What was a Ph.D.? Paper, nothing.

I had read all the usual – Ruskin, Byron, James, Mann – but none of it prepared me for Venice. Nothing can. If you can bring your life to Venice and it survives, then it's probably sound. My future crumbled in the air here. And I had thought it was solid.

We were flying BEA with a touch-down in Paris on the way back. We had a drink in the airport at Le Bourget. I had been morose for a day and a half, practically all of our wonderful weekend. Finally he asked if anything was wrong.

I said all kinds of things I didn't even know I thought. I had to be honest. I had to match up to Venice. He went to Wales and married a nice girl (they always do) and that was that.

Page 2 of 2

At the time I thought I was being brave; in fact I was just doing what I had no choice but to do. Regrets? None. Not even over unfulfilled motherhood? It finds other ways of fulfilling itself. No life is easy. You have to find the one for you. You try and you might be wrong, but at least you honour your gifts. That may be life's only injunction.

The most extraordinary thing happened in the church. The statue – did I already tell you? – smiled at me. I thought I was going mad, but it is a miraculous statue and the priest wasn't a bit surprised. Am I going soft in my old age? A palpitation, the head swims, the eyes mist over – that sort of thing? And the feeling is just a flush of well-being as good health returns? But my heart is fine. The doctor said so. I wish you could feel the love of Santa Monica. You are loved.

Loved, loved, loved,

Sally.

This was the last communication received from Sally Splinter. On the afternoon of Sunday May 15th she was discovered supine in the Lady Chapel of Santa Monica dell' Orto with a smile on her face, deceased of unknown causes.

Now that Jesus College has decided to take on Santa Monica for its 'Venice in Peril' Campaign, it is strongly hoped our donors will give generously to realize Sally's dream of saving Santa Monica. The campaign gratefully acknowledges the splendid contributions generated by Ms Gornick, now Mrs Owen, through her vigorous fundraising in Ohio.

Don't forget the Ball!

Ian McMillan

was born in 1956, and has been a freelance writer, performer and broadcaster since 1981.

He currently presents BBC Radio 3's The Verb every Friday night and makes documentaries for BBC Radio 4.

His work includes poetry, some serious, some hilarious, and short stories. He also writes comedy series for radio, plays for radio and the stage, and columns for publications ranging from the Barnsley Chronicle to The New Statesman.

He loves to collaborate with other artists and is currently working with photographers, cartoonists and musicians.

In 1997 he was awarded the newly created post of;

The Bard of Barnsley FC.

Ian says that this is a Life Peerage, and entitles him to a seat in The House of Lards.

The following story seems born of his true northern spirit.

Mr Mason's Story

On the first day, Mr Mason, on his way to work on the train, reached up and scratched his head and felt a spot there. A pimple. A sight disturbance under the hair. Something that could have been a pellet, or a peanut.

On the second day, Mr Mason, on his way home from the station, experienced a sharp pain at the top of his head where the pimple was. It was, he said to his wife, as though he was being stabbed with a fork. She looked puzzled. He qualified: a small fork, a small sharp fork.

On the third day, Mr Mason, digging in his garden, felt a shower of rain passing over the village. He decided to carry on digging as it was a warm day and the rain felt uncomplicatedly pleasant. He noticed drops specking his work-shirt and making the handle of his spade shine. When he went indoors for the kettle-on routine he glanced in a mirror and noticed that although parts of him were slightly damp, the top of his head was completely dry. This was because the pimple, the spot on his head, was spreading. It was becoming a flat disc. A flat disc of cloth. Instinctively he reached up to pull it off but he found that it was stuck. More than stuck: it was part of him. Growing.

On the fourth day, Mr Mason, not one to have headaches, had a headache. It rang in his skull like a cracked bell; it made him wince, it made him draw in his breath. He took a couple of tablets and swallowed them down hard, as though the violence of the swallowing of the tablets would make the headache cower. Instead, it grew. In the mirror he saw that the flat disc of cloth on his head was spreading, growing wider and heavier. He rang the Doctor and made an emergency appointment for the next day.

On the fifth day, the Doctor examined Mr Mason's head and went out of the consulting room and came back with three colleagues and went out again and came back in with another colleague and several people from the crowded waiting room.

The Doctor pointed to Mr Mason's head and cleared his throat. When the Doctor spoke, his voice was clear and authoritative. 'What he have here,' he said, clearly and authoritatively, 'is an example of a very rare disease. I have been in General Practice for many years and I have never seen this condition before. Ladies and gentlemen, we are in the presence of 'Flat Cap Head'. There was a pause, seemingly a pause in the steady movement of Time. Someone said, 'My husband had that. When he took his cap off his hair was flat as a mat and there was a red ring round his skull.'

The Doctor looked disdainful. 'Madam, that is simply a temporary condition. Flat Cap Head is permanent and incurable. Over a period of a few short weeks, a flat cap grows from the head of the sufferer until they become, to use the vernacular, All Cap.'

The silence wandered round the room, silently. A young man asked 'Is it a stylish or a trendy flat cap?'

Mr Mason began to weep. 'Is there really no cure?' he asked. The Doctor placed his trembling hand on Mr Mason's bony shoulder. 'I'm afraid not.' A voice piped up: 'I need a big walking cap for my new shop.'

On the seventeenth day, Mr Mason got dressed in front of the mirror although, to be honest, he didn't need to. When he looked in the mirror he saw a splendid flat cap that somehow redefined the word Jaunty and made it sparkle and shine.

Mr Mason liked to read books and he'd read Kafka's Metamorphosis, about the man who turned into a beetle, and he'd read David Garnett's Lady Into Fox about the lady who did just that, and it seemed that those stories often ended badly or inconclusively. His story wasn't ending like that. His story was ending well. Mr Mason had been employed as the Symbolic Mascot of his new friend Mr Scholes's Flat Cap Bazaar; a shop that sold Flat Caps of every kind from the wearable to the eatable to the sailable-in.

Mr Mason clambered into the taxi that Mr Scholes had laid on. He passed cheering crowds on the way to the bazaar and, after a while, with a prickling of the eyes, realised that the crowds were making lots of crowd-noises for him.

At the bazaar a brass band played and a choir sang a specially commissioned Flat Cap Cantata. A ribbon was there for him to snip. He snipped it and the cheering rose to a crescendo and beyond to two crescendos.

On the twenty-third day, Mr Mason reflected on his life. He was a celebrity, but he was also a flat cap. He had received lots of declarations of love and some threats but, were they really for him, or for his condition? Was he defined by his flat-cap-ness? People wanted to have their photographs taken with him and they asked him for autographs. He would say 'I'm only me. I'm the same as I ever was. It's just that now I'm a flat cap.' and people would laugh as though he'd said something really funny.

One the fifty-fourth day, Mr Mason woke up and he felt different; he couldn't feel the flat cap at all. He was back to how he was before! He began to sing a triumphant song. And woke himself up. And he was still a giant flat cap. And the life that had changed forever when he felt that pimple on the first day was still changed. Forever. Outside, birds, who were not flat caps, sang.

Jemma Kennedy

is a novelist, playwright and screenwriter. Her first novel 'Skywalking' was published in 2003 and she has been writing for the stage since 2004. She was awarded a Jerwood Arvon Young Playwright's Apprenticeship in 2006 and was Pearson Playwright in residence at the National Theatre in 2010.

Recent plays include 'The Prince and the Pauper' (Unicorn Theatre 2012), 'The Grand Irrationality' (Lost Theatre Studio, Los Angeles 2012), 'Don't Feed the Animals' (National Theatre Connections 2013), and 'The Summer Book', adapted from the novel by Tove Jansson (Unicorn Theatre, 2014).

She is currently under commission to the National Theatre where she teaches playwriting and has recently devised their New Views online playwriting course for young writers.

Jemma's first feature film, 'The Greatest Englishman' (Marathon Films, director Justin Hardy) is in post-production.

She is currently writing her second feature, 'Frozen' (Wellcome Trust development award) for director Amanda Boyle, and is shortly to adapt Barbara Pym's novel 'Excellent Women' for the BBC and Raindog Films.

Jemma is an avid traveller and waiter watcher. This short story was written on an artists' retreat outside Barcelona and is based on her experience in a famous Catalan restaurant.

Although Jemma can no longer remember which parts of the story are true and which parts she made up, the baseball cap and the techno definitely happened, and cast a shadow over the rest of her stay in Spain – the headwaiter haunts her to this day. She hopes to someday complete a collection of short stories about waiters she has known and loved around the world.

The Fig Tree

The restaurant was called La Figuera and was quite famous in the region, not least for the view from the terrace, with the jagged crown of Montserrat high above it and the olive groves falling in silvery waves to the horizon. In the centre of the terrace a vast fig tree grew. It was two hundred years old and a local landmark. People drove from Barcelona to eat the home-reared meat and cheese and drink the strong wine, crooked in the arm of the ancient mountain, shaded by the ancient tree.

I had come with Nette, a Norwegian girl of 22 who worked in my *hostal.* She was an overgrown farm girl, six feet tall, her limbs brown and solid as wood, her laugh sudden and happy. She knew how to drown kittens and to crochet, and was sleeping with the Italian water-colourist, a thin boy with thighs half the size of hers. In the afternoons she studied Spanish and drank beer with the locals, who had taught her how to curse in Catalan. Everybody loved her, especially the waiters at La Figuera.

There were nine or ten of them; the restaurant was large and got very busy in high season. Most of them were local men, along with some South Americans and a Cuban with a shaved head; all of them young and apparently indestructible, with an array of scars and tattoos and damaged teeth. One by one they came to our table to pay homage to Nette. One brought the basket of bread and tomatoes, another a carafe of wine, a third our plates of pork chops. She introduced each of them to me by name, and each in turn gave me a shy smile, then lowered his eyes to my breasts in a brief benediction.

It was good to be away from the *hostal* and the residents. Most had come to paint the landscape, others to sculpt or take photographs. They were all poor and eager and hungry, and went about their chores with a dogged efficiency that was quite unlike the daily sunlit meanderings I'd glimpsed in the communal artist studios, where they worked on 'showings' that never quite materialized. I was poor myself, and a writer, or so I imagined, but I kept myself apart, wary of the cluttered communal kitchen and its grubby internationalism; the flirting, the arguments, the sharing of cheap food and cheaper wine. They thought me unfriendly, I knew, but I wasn't ready to join their brotherhood yet. I had an excuse – a broken heart – and I consoled myself with the idea that my loneliness was somehow nobler than their endless couplings and regroupings.

After the first week people left me alone, except for Nette, whose job it was to collect the rent and supply the greyish sheets and towels, and who seemed impervious to any emotional state that didn't mirror her own, which was unchangingly bland and cheerful as milk. Tonight she had persuaded me to visit the local restaurant, as the others had gone on a hike, and it was Friday night, and her young blood told her that a ritual celebration was in order. We had walked there through the dusty olive groves, a ragged dog trotting behind us for the last mile, and the calcified fingers of the mountain beckoning us on as the sun sank inch by inch and finally disappeared, casting the valley into shadow.

In the calm twilight we ate and drank while Nette regaled me with stories of her lovers back in Norway. The blonde farm worker with the huge misshapen hands who wept like a child at climax; the middle-aged painter for whom she posed naked on dustsheets stained with linseed oil; the waiter at the Mexican restaurant who called her *mi cielo* – my sky – and only wanted her from behind. Always these waiters, I said, as the gold-toothed Argentine presented a bowl of hazelnuts and poured the thick dessert wine. We laughed, but it was hard not to feel a little jaded in the sturdy shade of Nette's physical contentment with life, with her robust appetites so easily sated. I had fled to Spain when my own affair ended and had let nobody touch me for six months. I couldn't shake the memory of Michael's hands, his mouth; I felt the broken chains of physical intimacy more keenly than I did the spent rhetoric of love. Somehow the crude messiness of life at the *hostal* was a constant reminder of him. Communal sinks, drying socks, the blackened cooking pots on the stove; all of them seemed to share his DNA and debase me.

But now I was drunk, and the air was cool, and I felt better. Slowly the restaurant emptied. There were Spanish families on holiday, German walkers with crampons and rucksacks, a table of young Swedish men with blunt fair beards and the serene expressions of philosophers as yet untainted by the cynical discovery that life was not entirely of their own making. Nette and I sat on, batting away the moths that formed a fluttering halo around the lamp. She pointed out the headwaiter, who was called Joan. He was over fifty; short and squat and bowlegged, but he moved with incredible speed and elegance over the terrace with his heavy tray, barking commands in Spanish and Catalan. At length he came to our table and hovered over us.

'Sit down,' Nette commanded, and he bowed his head and obeyed. Nette told him my name. '*Escritura Inglesa*,' she added with a proprietorial air, and the waiter's eyes widened. He nodded sagely and shook my hand. His palm was warm and alive, like the *jamón ibérico* we had eaten before. I waited for the quick salutation to my chest, but it didn't come. Instead he said something in Spanish that I didn't understand.

Nette said, 'If he wasn't a waiter, he would have liked to be a writer,' and the man nodded again and eyed me shyly.

He stayed and had a glass with us, and his eyes danced between us like the moths, more often alighting on my face, which pleased me unexpectedly. By now we were the only customers left and when they had closed the restaurant the waiters sat down to their evening meal. We joined them at their table, where the fig tree was its thickest, the great twisted trunk encased in a brick chimney two feet tall. Plates of cheese and meat and bread were brought from the kitchen, and the men ate with gusto and drank the owner's wine with many toasts to Catalonia and the mother countries of the immigrants. The headwaiter ate little, but smoked and sipped a glass of brandy, watching the other men benignly. He passed me a morsel of cheese and waited for me to swallow it. When I nodded my appreciation, his face contracted with pleasure.

The Cuban made a comment and the men laughed like children, their cheeks pink with excitement.

'He wants to know if you have cows in England,' Nette said, and her smile was wide and forgiving. I smiled too, but I caught the headwaiter's eye, and his face was sober. He spoke to his men in rapid Catalan and the laughter tailed away. The talk soon turned to football, and I relaxed and sipped some brandy.

Nette leaned towards me, her breath warm against my face. 'Joan is very worried they have offended you. He offers his apologies.'

I smiled once more at the headwaiter, whose brown eyes were fixed on me anxiously. '*De nada*,' I said, and shrugged to show I could take a joke. I waited for him to smile back but he merely inclined his head – a small movement but one that was full of dignity, and I felt that I was the one who should apologize. He came and sat next to me then, and I asked him about the fig tree.

'Very old,' he said in English. 'Many years. A tree for great luck.'

I looked at his bare knee beneath the hem of the shorts he had changed into, the skin dark and rough, his feet now squashed into rubber sandals. I began to question him about the restaurant, about his work and his life in the region, and he thought carefully before making his answers. In the light from the hanging lantern I examined the broken red veins on his cheeks and the silver in his thinning hair as though I was making a map of him, laying down each detail with great attention and care. Nette translated when I didn't understand. He was born in a village a few miles west, had worked in the restaurant since he was twenty and watched it grow from a small family business into one that was written about in culinary magazines in Europe and America. The fine lines on his face softened as he spoke, and I saw the sinews in his arms and, when he drew on his cigarette, that his nails were bitten to the quick. He talked about the mountain, its moods and shadows; about the vines below it, and the monastery beyond it where the monks sang unseen, their hymns echoing across the ravine. He glanced at me often to gauge my reaction, and I kept on listening and watching, and for each line I added to the map of him one of my own lines was erased, leaving a cool blankness where the spoiled and jagged marks had lain. The leaves of the fig tree drooped over us, dark and waxy. Across from us the other waiters were now singing tunelessly about love and glory, and the jug of wine was almost empty.

The headwaiter smiled at me. 'They sing *amor*,' he said, and Nette nudged me with her great brown elbow, laughter spilling from her like stuffing from a pillow.

'Joan has a fancy for you,' she whispered, and poured the last of the wine into her glass. I saw her tongue flash out and catch the final drops, joyful and unashamed, and I didn't envy her any longer. Her knee was pressing against mine, a warm bolster of flesh, and on the other side was the headwaiter's thin leg and the neon orange shorts, and I felt hemmed in by her happiness and his shyness and his pride. For the first time Michael was far away, and his hands were tethered to his sides and couldn't reach out to touch me.

The cheese was gone now, and the bread, and empty cigarette packets littered the table. One by one the waiters left, drunk and unsteady, calling out their farewells. It was after two, and the moon was high and unflinching. The headwaiter held a whispered conversation with Nette, and then inclined his head towards me in patient deference.

'Joan will drive us home,' Nette said, and nudged me again. I smiled at the small man, and thanked him. As a parting gift, he pressed a fresh fig into each of our palms, and tucked a cigarette behind Nette's ear.

We walked down the steps into the car park, the headwaiter hurrying ahead on his dancer's feet, still clutching his brandy glass. The car was a Fiat, newish, and smelled of upholstery and stale tobacco. A pair of football boots lay on the floor, and a tin of shaving foam. I sat in the back, although I felt he would have preferred me to go in front, but Nette's legs were longer than mine, and we laughed about this as he brushed off the back seat with the flat of his hand. Then he adjusted his seat and put on a yellow baseball cap and started the engine. Techno music blasted out of the speakers behind my head, rupturing the night silence. He turned his head as he reversed, sending up sprays of gravel.

'You like the music?' he asked, and I could only nod and smile, although I felt obscurely cheated. As we pulled away I looked back at the restaurant and I could see the silhouette of the fig tree outlined against the pale mountain.

Nette was lurching about in time to the music – she had moved effortlessly into this strange newness – and she lit her cigarette and passed me back the brandy glass. I took a sip and my teeth clicked against the glass, but it was drowned out by the radio. The DJ let out a burst of florid Catalan and another techno track started up. The headwaiter drove one-handed, nodding his head to the diabolical music, the peak of his yellow cap bobbing about like a fairground target. I held on to the handle above the passenger window and felt the air on my hot cheeks. He kept gazing at me in the rear view mirror as he had done under the fig tree, and I felt the terrible pull of his longing and his desire to please me, but now it made me feel small and mean. I wanted his other self back – the one who had inclined his head and waited to hear me speak, the one who was proud of his job and the wines and the cheese.

In the front they were discussing whether or not he should come into the *hostal* for a nightcap. Nette was drunk and her Spanish was loud and garbled, and I suddenly felt a great silence descend, blocking out the techno and their voices and the sound of the night rushing by. I was hearing the silence in the kitchen of the *hostal*, where the headwaiter and I would sit opposite each other at the scarred oak table, with the crumbs and smears of the other guests' dinners covering it, and flies walking between them, and the bare bulb overhead illuminating everything. I saw how the map I had drawn was all wrong – that beneath the harsh light the lines on his skin would cut deeper and the hollows in his skull be more exposed, and that under the table his thin legs would be ridiculous in the orange shorts he had bought in a local town and tried on before a mirror and paid for with the money he had earned at the restaurant under the mountain.

'Not tonight,' I said. 'I have to sleep.' It carried over the techno, and then they both fell silent, and stayed that way for the rest of the journey.

He pulled the car up outside the *hostal* and we got out. Nette thanked him thickly and kissed both his cheeks and lumbered off towards the front porch. I walked around to the open car window. The empty brandy glass lay in his lap and the yellow cap sat on his head at a rakish angle. I said goodbye in formal Spanish. He nodded and put the car into gear. As he pulled away he looked back at me and his eyes glittered in his tired face. I could hear the speakers pounding as the car drove away too fast, the wheels skidding, and I thought of his white face on the highway and of his small flat; a narrow bed with synthetic sheets, all far away from the cool green shade of the fig tree.

I stood there listening to the grating of the cicadas, and I heard Nette on the stairs inside. She was going to look for the Italian. The kitchen lights were on and I decided to go there. I hoped someone else was up, someone I could talk to. I was still holding the warm fig.

Judith Allnatt

is an acclaimed short story writer and novelist. Her first novel, 'A Mile of River', was a Radio 5 Live Book of the Month and was shortlisted for the Portico Prize for Literature.

Her second novel, 'The Poet's Wife', was shortlisted for the East Midlands Book Award.

Judith's short stories have featured in the Bridport Prize Anthology, the Commonwealth Short Story Awards, and on BBC Radio 4.

Her new novel, 'The Moon Field', described by The Times as 'deeply moving', is set in the First World War.

Judith has lectured widely on Creative Writing, both for universities and freelance, for almost two decades.

She lives with her family in Northamptonshire and is working on her fourth novel.

Her contribution to this anthology is the following story, 'Black Widow'.

Black Widow

Will was driving home from Heathrow on a dark, wet February evening, the last leg of his journey from a business trip to Paris. He drove with his lights on full beam to clear the fast lane ahead of him so that his Porsche had the clear run he felt she deserved, his boyish enthusiasm for speed heightened by the elation he felt at having been offered the job he'd been angling for.

'It'll mean a lot more travel' he thought, 'I must brush up on my languages.' For the first time he felt uncomfortable as he imagined telling this part of the good news to Caroline. He had meant to ring her from France, between the meetings and the wining and dining - try to put things right between them after their row.

Her usual grumbles had come out: he was always away, he'd forgotten their anniversary again, he didn't spend enough time with the kids, oh yes, and she'd wanted him to be at some swimming gala.

'It's not for me, Will, it's for Lauren. She's been practicing for ages because she thought you were coming.'

Then, when he'd tried to explain: 'God! What does she have to do to get an hour of your attention?'

And there was the party he'd had to miss.

Caroline was going to wear her black dress, her favourite, a fitted black velvet number with a deep scoop neckline. She'd been mending a tiny split in the seam and the dress lay across her knees in soft, lustrous folds. The light from the lamp had glittered on the jewellery she'd laid out ready and on her sewing things: reels of thread, scissors and pin cushion.

When he'd said he had to go abroad and couldn't make it after all, she'd thrown the dress aside.

'So I have to go on my own again,' she'd said, staring at him defiantly, '...dressed appropriately in my widow's weeds.'

He'd walked out of the room.

He flashed his lights at the car up ahead and put his foot down as it moved over, trying to recapture his victorious mood. The lights that had been filling his mirror dropped back, then pulled close again. He eased his foot further down until they dropped away behind him.

Caroline would be all right. She had cooled off enough to pack his case after all, although her goodbye had been rather tight lipped. She would have come round by now.

He thought of her waiting, watching TV, his favourite dinner in the oven, a bottle of wine beside her on the coffee table with an extra glass set ready for him.

'Junction 13'. The familiar sign caught his eye and he realised with a shock that he was right on top of the turning for home. He pulled across and indicated simultaneously, swerving between two cars and across the white hatching. He braked as he hit the slip road, his tyres squealing on the wet, greasy surface. He felt the back of the car slew to the left and then a bone-shaking thud as metal met metal.

He skidded, yanked the wheel around and careered to a stop, ending up miraculously pointing in more or less the right direction before the road met the roundabout. He let out a deep breath. He had banged his head pretty hard but that was all.

He tried to undo his seatbelt. 'Why won't the bloody thing come undone!'

He felt almost tearful; his hands wouldn't seem to do what he wanted. 'Calm down,' he thought. 'You're all in one piece.'

The seatbelt finally gave with a click.

He climbed out of the Porsche and saw the headlights of the other car pointing crazily up the bank. He started to walk unsteadily towards it, feeling sick with apprehension as he saw the shattered windscreen, and then began to run as he smelt the petrol that was leaking from the fractured tank.

Inside the car, a young man was slumped over the steering wheel, the radio still crackling and spitting.

Will hauled him out and dragged him clear. He laid him on the grass under a lamppost's garish orange light. He was breathing, but his arm hung limply at a strange angle. His face was cut and bruised and his hair was darkened with blood on one side of his head. Will rang the ambulance and police and gingerly put his jacket over the young man.

He sat down beside him, the rain soaking through his thin shirt making it cling. Now and then a car swished past but no one stopped.

'The world can be a cold kind of place,' Will thought.

'You'd better come, too,' said the policeman, holding the ambulance door open. 'You've had a nasty shock. Check up at the General first, statement later, ok?'

Will climbed in and the ambulance pulled away. He watched blankly as the paramedic rigged the young man up to a drip then turned to talk to the driver through the open partition. 'The head wound's nasty,' he was saying, '...and there's a broken collar bone and ribs need sorting too. Better move it, Mike.'

The ambulance re-joined the motorway, blue light flashing. Will stared at the road ahead.

'My God, I've been lucky,' Will thought. 'That could have been it. The end of everything.'

Suddenly he found he wanted Caroline very much, to have her put her arms around him, to see her smile, to be close like they were in the old days.

Shakily, he put his hand to his aching head and gazed at the headlights and taillights ahead as the streams of cars swooped down into the valley and climbed the other side.

Like a beautiful necklace, he thought: diamonds one way and rubies the other and the night is running it through her fingers in the lap of her black dress...

He tried to concentrate. Things were becoming confused. The policeman was talking to him but he couldn't seem to take in the words. The policeman took off his hat and scratched his head as if nonplussed, then laid the hat upside down on his knees. He said something else that Will couldn't make out. Will made an effort to hold his attention steady.

'All right, Sir?

He nodded.

'Better not go to sleep, Sir. Could be a bit concussed you know. Come on now, you talk to me. Tell me your full name and address for starters.'

Will told him and he jotted it down in his notebook.

'Right then, what about the other guy? Let's have a look in his pockets for some ID.'

He pulled out the young man's wallet and emptied a jumble of bank notes and odds and ends into his upturned hat. He sifted through the contents, looking for a driver's licence.

Will stared. He leaned across and pulled the policeman's hand out of the way. On the top of the pile was a photo of Caroline.

Caroline in her black dress.

Smiling.

Julia South

is 59 and writing has always been an important part of her life. She has an MA in Creative Writing from Sheffield Hallam University which gave her the impetus to write her first novel, although the main area of her work is in short story.

Julia enjoys getting together with other writers in classes and workshops, where she often ends up writing pieces that surprise her.

'Mortal' was written as an experiment to see if it was possible to sustain a whole story using the second person (the 'you' voice), while exploring that moment in a relationship when a lover falls from grace.

Julia is a lesbian, and writes often about her experiences in a world where to be lesbian is still to be an 'outsider', even in these days of gay marriage. In her stories, she tries to honour the richness of lesbian experience and to encourage others to empathise with lesbian characters.

Julia's work in the public and charitable sectors has involved the writing of case studies, a special source of enjoyment, exploring the impact of project work on the lives of other people.

Julia lives in Sheffield with her partner, Sue, who she met on a writing course 27 years ago.

Mortal

You're in Arcadia, where cockerels strut through olive groves and children play tag by white, stone cottages. You're on holiday with Avril, driving back from Olympia. The site had swarmed with Americans off a cruise liner, but you hadn't minded. You'd charged around the stadium in the full sun like some female Adonis.

Now the sun is setting, blood red on the horizon. Avril is driving. You like glancing across at her profile, her obvious concentration. Every so often she utters an expletive as a goat lurches onto a boulder by the road, or the bend is sharp. You admire her nerve. You're glad you don't drive, don't have to prove yourself, can look about at the languorous hills, the far glint of sea.

You've just passed a shrine, seen the wick burning in it. You imagine an old Greek woman in black labouring up the hillside to renew the oil, to say prayers for a dead son or husband. On this lonely road. You shiver very slightly. You think of the transience of love, of joy, of the woman's constancy. And you reach across with your hand and touch your lover's head. Her hair is very short, fine, silky to your touch. She bends her head back into your hand. And you can imagine no moment more perfect than now – driving back from Olympia and the sun setting and the smell of cooking drifting towards you from the villages, and another week to go.

You might not have noticed. You don't have to watch the road as Avril does. But it catches your eye. A faint scurry ahead, on the right-hand side, in amongst the undergrowth. Something reddish tan. You think it might be a fox. You've seen one already – burnished gold – surveying the scene up on the hillside. But no, this isn't a fox. It's a dog. A stray, Avril says afterwards. Just a stray. A gangly, rust-coloured mutt that has shot into the road, yelping in panic or stupid playfulness, careering towards the car.

'Get over, Avril' you shout. 'For fuck's sake, get over!' But it's too late. Avril swerves. The brakes squeal. The car lurches to the left, but not in time. There's a pitiless mushing against the back wheel. The yelping has stopped. Avril is fighting with the steering wheel to regain control. Then you're back on the other side of the road, driving on.

You turn, look through the back window.

'It'll be dead,' Avril says.

There's a lump on the road. It might have been a piece of old sacking dropped from a truck.

'Stop!'

You swing back round to face her. 'Please! It could still be alive.'

'I can't,' she shouts. 'Not here. It's dangerous.'

'But we can't just leave it.'

The road is narrow, lined with olive groves.

'What about here?' You point to a scrubby bank on the left-hand side.

'We've no insurance for the chassis. Don't you remember?'

You say nothing. The sun has gone and she drives more slowly now. Soon you are down in the valley, driving the last stretch along a main road lined with plastic greenhouses. They slide past and you feel smothered by the falling darkness. It's so fast here.

'Where do you fancy eating tonight?' she asks, at the first sign for the resort. The outskirts are piled with rough-built, concrete houses advertising 'rooms for rent'. Some are draped in bougainvillea.

'I'm not hungry,' you reply. 'I don't think I'll bother.'

'For god's sake,' she says. 'It was an accident. Don't you think I'm upset as well.'

She knows you're not any sort of animal lover. You throw stones at the neighbour's cat when it comes into the garden.

But this is not about the dog. How come you never saw it before? That flintiness in Avril's face. The hard set to her jaw.

You stupid cow.

'I don't get it,' she says, as you maintain your stand and call at the dingy, corner shop to buy bread and cheese to have in the room. 'I didn't mean to kill the dog. Don't you think I wish I hadn't? But I've done nothing to you.'

And you shrug and think: I could rescue her. I could say, 'I'm being silly. I'm sorry.' Back in the room, which has been freshly swept, the beds newly made, you could take her in your arms and kiss her and say: 'Let's forget what happened. It must have been horrible for you too.'

But you don't. You want to. You recall the time – had you just made love? – when Avril, leaning over you, had said: 'Will I go the way of all the others?' And you'd pulled her to you. You remember the heat of her. And you'd told her it would never happen.

'I'm going to have a proper meal,' she says, as she empties out the contents of her rucksack onto the bed. 'Even if you don't want to.'

She's like that. It's what you like about her. The feistiness. The refusal to get drawn down. Except now such qualities are linked in your mind to a certain callousness, a preparedness to leave a still-warm creature to be pummelled on the road. And she gets undressed and has a shower and changes into her blue silk top and you don't say anything. You need her help, but she doesn't know that.

Out she goes. You watch her from the balcony. She's a solitary figure amongst the groups of people, the couples. She's heading, you guess, for Zorba's, the taverna you like on the front. She looks vulnerable down there in the darkness all on her own, her rucksack thrown over one shoulder.

If she had turned and waved or even looked up at you, you might have changed your mind and gone down to join her. But she never turns back, never looks round. She stops under the street lamp, where the dirt path to the house meets the tarmac road.

Steve and Mo are there, the couple from downstairs who tell you in such detail what they've been up to. She seems to be laughing at something they have said to her. God forbid she seems to be joining them, to be walking off with them.

You need a drink. You pour yourself a large glass of ouzo. There's no ice. Water will have to do. You rip off a hunk of bread, which you eat with crumbly feta cheese. You sit on the balcony, prey to mosquitos, and watch the trickle of people coming up and down the path and along the road. You get very drunk. Cicadas thrum in the undergrowth around the building. And she doesn't return. You finish all the bread and cadge a cigarette from a man on an adjoining balcony who wants to make conversation, but you fob him off. You want to be alone. Can't he bloody see that?

Then, when you've almost given up waiting and the ouzo is all gone, Avril turns up. You hadn't even spotted her coming down the path.

'Well that was unexpectedly enjoyable,' she says through the balcony door as she strips off her blue top. 'There's more to Steve and Mo than we thought.'

Is she out of her mind? But you cannot deny that you are pleased she is back and it pierces the drunken blur, this knowledge that you're pleased, that she is found again.

Later, in the darkness, she reaches a hand across the gap between the two, freshly laundered beds. It is the first night that neither she nor you have thought to push them together. And you can think of no reason not to give her your hand and let her take it and kiss the fingers one by one.

'Are we friends?' she asks.

'S'pose so.'

And sleep claims you and you don't remember her returning your hand, but she must have, because it is morning and she is not in her bed. She is up and running a tap to fill the kettle. Then she's pushing open the shutters and light floods the room.

'What a glorious day!' she declares, standing in the open door to the balcony, looking out at the sea. As if nothing has happened. As if there isn't now a rent, a hair fracture, in that perfect view.

Kirstin Zhang

was brought up in Papua New Guinea during one of the worst droughts in its history. She now lives on the west coast of Scotland and never complains about the rain.

Following studies at Keio University, Tokyo, and the School of Oriental & African Studies, Kirstin completed a MLitt in Creative Writing at the University of Glasgow and was subsequently mentored by the author Romesh Gunesekera.

Winner of The Scotsman and Orange Short Fiction Prize (her winning entry, 'The Enemy Within', is Kirstin's contribution to this anthology) and 2014's Fish Short Memoir Prize, her works of fiction have appeared in various publications, including GQ, Soho House Magazine and The Scotsman. She is currently working on a short story collection 'In Their Song', set in Japan during the dying days of the Pacific War.

The inspiration for 'The Enemy Within' was a picture in the *Guardian* of men spraying against dengue fever in Indonesia, and a short article about the upcoming elections there.

In 1965, the slaughter of nearly one million suspected Communists during an army coup by General Suharto was largely ignored by the Western press, and is still not widely discussed in Indonesia itself. Many more potential victims have lived for nearly thirty years alongside their enemy, always watching, always waiting to be discovered...

The Enemy Within

Akbar scuffed at the dry soil with his sandals. They were in for another drought. Peanut plants drooped in the heat. The fruit on the pawpaw trees hung low on the skinny trunks, reminding Akbar of the worn village women of his youth. The dog that lay beneath the front step didn't even lift its nose from the dirt as Akbar made his way towards the house.

He'd had a dog as a boy. It would follow every handful of tapioca from Akbar's bowl to his mouth. Without fail, Akbar would fling the bowl to the ground and shout,

'That look's enough to put you off your food.'

The dog's thin body would flinch and then his stubby tail would wriggle in pleasure as it worked off the sticky scabs of tapioca from the inside of the bowl. Akbar wondered what had happened to that dog.

The old lady listened to him patiently.

'You don't understand,' he said, 'It's a matter of life and death.'

He pointed to the poster stuck to the van; a giant mosquito caught within a rifle's crosshairs. Under it in red-

'Dengue: the enemy within.'

'One million IDRs is not a lot to keep your family healthy,' he added, studiously avoiding the gaze of the children with the sticky eyes who hung around her legs.

The official charge was less but so far no one had objected. It helped that the national radio station ran a continuous tally of the afflicted. You didn't need to read to know that already three hundred victims of the fever had been cremated, a thousand suspected cases had been hospitalised and there were now claims that supplies of the chemicals used to destroy the mosquito nests were running low.

The old woman blinked towards the van.

One of the children sniffed.

Akbar put his hand into his shirt pocket and took out two pieces of caramel. Sighing, he held the candy out to the children.

They looked at the old woman.

She blinked with her watery eyes at Akbar.

'Ok, I can spray for eighty.'

The woman nodded to the children. They took the candy.

Akbar waved to the two men in the truck and they clambered out of the vehicle looking like extras from a western – bandanas tied around their faces to protect against the fumes of the chemicals.

As Akbar opened the passenger door, one of them, Jimmy, muttered, 'I wouldn't live in a dump like that, even if I was a mosquito.'

Akbar stopped and patted Jimmy's partner on the back, 'Hey, Tata, you're not looking too hot. Must be the fumes. Why don't you sit this one out?' Jimmy began to unload the gear alone, muttering all the while.

Once they were both back in the van, Tata took out a piece of dried squid from the glove box and began to suck on it, 'So what'd you get?' he asked.

Akbar rolled down the window, 'I wish you wouldn't eat that stuff. It stinks up the van.'

He put his elbow on the window frame and watched Jimmy kick the dog from under the steps.

'So what did you get?' Tata repeated. He had started on a second piece of squid.

'Seventy,' replied Akbar.

'Seventy?'

Akbar fished a handful of crumpled notes out of his shirt pocket, took two for himself, handed two to Tata and put the rest into a plastic wallet. Jimmy got nothing; it was their little secret.

'We got Habibie tomorrow. We'll get plenty there.'

He thought of Habibie, where houses spilled out into bougainvillea-filled gardens. Those houses belonged to people who could afford to run the air conditioning just for their Persian cat.

The dog had sought shade under one of the pawpaw trees and stood rubbing its back with its nose, pink and black mottled flesh showing through thinning grey hair.

Akbar fingered the plastic wallet on his lap. If his wife was in a good mood when he got home he'd ask her about getting a dog. He'd tell her that there was a rapist on the loose. He'd say he was not leaving her at home without proper security. He'd really play it up.

Jimmy was done.

The old lady and the children stood watching him walk back to the truck. The children waved to Akbar.

Hey, it could be true, Akbar thought. He waved back.

There were a lot of bad people out there.

When he got home that evening, he found his wife mopping the floor and the contents of the fridge lying on the table.

'I'm going to my brother's,' she said, and as she reached the bottom of the stairs she shouted without turning, 'And don't think I'm sharing a bed with a man who couldn't care less if I died of food poisoning.'

Akbar kicked the fridge – it usually did the trick – but the rusting heap simply shuddered and fell back into silence.

Akbar changed back into his sandals and ate dinner at the café round the corner.

By the time he returned, his wife was already asleep. He pulled a futon from a cupboard in the front room and lay down without changing out of his clothes. But sleep was not restful. In his dreams giant mosquitoes hovered over a paddy field. Suddenly a voice from the dark shouted, 'Quick… spray the bastards now.'

There was a rattle of gunfire and mosquitoes began to drop amongst the rice plants.

'We'll never be safe until we kill them all,' called another voice.

There was more gunfire and then silence. In his dream, Akbar waited for a long time and then crept out from his hiding place. He felt the ice of water creep around his ankles… the dead mosquitoes lay face down in the stagnant pool. He picked up a planting stick which was floating nearby and prodded one. The mosquito body bobbed right side up. It had the face of his father. Akbar woke himself with a shout.

'Is it not enough that I can't eat in my own house, but now you shout the place down?'

His wife had snapped on the light and was stood at the door.

Akbar sat blinking. 'I was dreaming,' he murmured.

His wife peered at him through puffy eyes, 'Dreams are for those with a guilty conscience,' and flicked off the electricity.

Unable to sleep, Akbar got up. In the kitchen he made some barley tea and stood drinking it as he looked out through the mesh door. Outside, a few people moved about like spectres in the grey light of early morning. Draining the last of the warm liquid between his teeth, he glanced back towards the dark interior of the house and slid his feet into his sandals.

His work unit was a fifteen-minute walk from the house and lay beside a river which came up from the sea. Sometimes salt-water crocodiles or even basking sharks could be seen floating along amongst the tall weeds.

Akbar was half way across the bridge when he saw something sitting at the far end, just where the walkway split into two; one following the bank towards the main mosque and the other leading up to the back gate of his work place - the City Health and Cleansing Department. As he got closer, he realised that it was a large cardboard box. He slid one of his hands into a slot in the side, aiming to fling it into the nearest skip, and felt the contents move with a surprising weight.

Laying the box back down, he opened it slowly. Tata had once found a boa constrictor asleep in a bucket under a house they had sprayed. Inside the box lay three puppies. At first glance all three seemed dead but, as Akbar stared down at them, one stuck out a little pink tongue and began to make a sucking movement. Akbar quickly folded down the flaps of the box again and carried it through the gates and into the yard of the Health and Cleansing Department. Only the man who worked the furnace was around at this time so Akbar knew he wasn't likely to meet anyone.

He left the box in a small storeroom behind the toilet block and went to look for some gloves.

After disposing of the two dead puppies, he thoroughly checked the remaining one for ticks and fleas. It seemed remarkably clean. He took off the gloves and ran his fingers over the black fur. The puppy opened its eyes and peered at him. Its little mouth began to move again.

'We need to get you some food little man.'

In the canteen he found the remains of a carton of soya milk. He dripped this into the tiny mouth.

By the time he had finished feeding the puppy and had fashioned it a bed of torn newspaper, it was six o'clock. He ran his hand over the soft fur one more time and then shut the door to the storeroom behind him.

'You look like shit,' Tata stood slurping rice porridge in the canteen. 'Sleeping alone again?'

Akbar poured a glass of coffee and sat down at a table.

'Not eating?'

Akbar shook his head.

'After Habibie you'll be able to get the old lady her fridge, eh?'

Akbar quickly looked around to see if there was anyone else about and threw Tata a look.

'Talking of marital strife,' continued Tata, between mouthfuls of porridge, 'Did you hear about the man who strangled his sixteen stone wife and then tried to commit suicide by cutting off his penis? Front page of the Daily.'

Akbar sat nursing his coffee as Tata went back up for more porridge. He wondered why the man had chosen to strangle his wife. Surely there were easier ways to kill a woman – with insecticide, for one.

Tata returned with more porridge and a plate of pickles.
'Can you imagine..?'

Akbar could not.

'The Daily said it was obviously a protest at the emasculation of men today.'

Akbar would have smiled, but he felt suddenly weary. He laid his head on his folded arms. His brother-in-law worked for one of the big pharmaceutical companies - in sales - they supplied chemicals to the Health and Cleansing Department. He had used his contacts to get Akbar a job nearly ten years ago. Before that, Akbar had sweated from one manual job to the next. On a building site no one was interested in where you had come from.

'Come on sleeping beauty,' Tata slammed the table with his open palm and made Akbar jump. 'We got to go get those bloodsuckers - before they get us.'

On the way back to the department from Habibie, Akbar asked Tata to make a detour. They pulled up outside a well-known discount warehouse and Akbar spent fifteen minutes looking at fridges.

Jimmy, who always carried a transistor with him, sat in the back shaking his fist in time to the beat.

'Going to keep that down,' Akbar nodded as he clambered back in to the van, 'I got a real bad head.' He laid his cheek against the window. The glass was hot and he could feel the boom, boom, boom of the blood coursing through his brain.

Tata and Jimmy immediately prepared lunch on return to the office; great bowls of cold noodles in a broth with a thick skin of fat and fine sliced green onions. Akbar felt sick and went to sit in the toilet. The old ceramic bowl was cool against his skin. He flicked through a newspaper that someone had left on the floor. It was mostly about the fever. There was also coverage of the upcoming elections. He was scanning the list of candidates when his eye caught an article:

'The ghost of '65 still haunts many, but Indonesia must accept all its brothers if we are to enjoy a democratic society.'

Akbar heard the flap of rubber slippers in the corridor and then recognized the legs of Tata from under the door. Tata rocked to and fro creating little pockets of air between his meaty soles and the rubber. Now and then these escaped in tiny gasps. There was then the sound of a steady stream against porcelain.

Suddenly Akbar felt as if someone had poured a bucket of ice water over his head, and let out a groan.

'You in there, Akbar?'

With effort Akbar managed to reply, 'Stomach cramp.'

'What you need is good home-cooking,' Tata answered, 'The sooner you get that new fridge the better.'

After ten minutes the cramp had eased off. His hair was damp around his temples and he doused his face with cool water from the sink. When he left the toilets he turned towards the storeroom. Most of the men were having lunch and he might not have another chance to check on the puppy before it was time to head home.

The puppy began to whistle gently when it heard the door.

'Do you want to get us into trouble?' Akbar whispered.

He lifted the puppy out of the box and sat down on the floor. Beneath him the cement was cold and he shivered.

'We're going to have to find you a better home than this.'

The tiny dog buried its nose into Akbar's lap.

Perhaps he could get an allotment and keep the dog there. There were places you could rent further along the river. He knew his wife would never allow a dog into the house and there was no garden to put a kennel.

Maybe he'd think about it later; his head had begun to pound again. He flicked his tongue over his top lip. Akbar had never really been ill in his life but he had cheated death.

His family, like most peasants, had been members of the communist party. After the failed coup of nineteen sixty-five, Suharto's army had been quick to retaliate. As a regional party representative, Akbar's father had been taken away immediately.

When news emerged that the daughter of one of the kidnapped generals had been killed during the debacle, the army came back looking for younger blood. Akbar had hidden amongst the thin plants and ice water of the paddy. As the soldiers approached the house the dog had begun a ferocious barking.

In Bali, a barking dog warned of the presence of evil spirits and, perhaps superstitious, the soldiers backed off and left. Shortly afterwards, Akbar had left too.

Beads of sweat were beginning to gather in the folds around his nose and around the creases of his mouth. The dog had wriggled along Akbar's legs and was nearly at his ankles. He leant forward to retrieve the dog and suddenly felt himself falling into a faint.

Tiny as the little dog's whine was, it was enough to lead Tata to him when Akbar failed to return from the toilet. It was two o'clock and they were due to head out on another job.

Akbar lay delirious from the dengue fever, muttering about giant mosquitoes and 'killing the bastards before they got you.'

When he opened his eyes he found Tata sitting beside the bed.

'It's just as well I can keep a secret.'

Akbar tried to speak but his tongue hung loose against his lips.

'What do you think your wife would say if she knew?'

'His wife knew what?' Akbar's wife materialised beside them.

'New fridge,' he managed to mumble.

Akbar's wife looked at Tata.

'He's ordered you a new fridge,' said Tata.

Akbar's wife almost smiled. She leant against the wall, taking the weight off her swollen feet, and began to suck contentedly on the can of iced coffee she had taken from her bag.

Akbar groped at the cotton sheet and pulled it further up around his neck.

Tata bent his head to say goodbye and whispered, 'I'll take care of the little matter till you're fighting fit and ready to take on the enemy again.'

He pointed his fingers towards a poster on the wall warning about the Dengue, and discharged two imaginary pistols.

Lesley Glaister

is the author of thirteen novels; including:

'Honour Thy Father'

(winner of both Somerset Maugham and Betty Trask Awards)

'Limestone and Clay'

(Yorkshire Post's Author of the Year Award)

'Easy Peasy'

(shortlisted for the Guardian Fiction prize)

'Nina Todd has Gone' and, most recently,

'Little Egypt'

Lesley has written drama for Radio 4 and her first stage play was performed at the Crucible Studio Theatre in 2004.

She has also had numerous short stories anthologised and broadcast on BBC Radio 4 and has edited a book of women's short stories.

Lesley is a Fellow of the Royal Society of Literature and has taught creative writing at several universities. She currently works at St Andrews.

She lives in Edinburgh - with frequent sorties to Orkney – with her husband and dog.

Gorilla

They kissed. She didn't even know his name. The kiss was unexpected, unasked for, almost accidental.

Laughing at someone else's joke, they had both reached for their drinks at the same instant, their faces coming so close there seemed nothing else to do but kiss, as if being that close and not kissing would have been rude.

It was a long, soft and sizzling kiss. They pulled apart, his eyes glittering at her in the smoky light. She was speechless, embarrassed but unable to break his gaze. There was no intention there, she thought, it was a spontaneous act, a spark lit, not quite combustion.

Someone else spoke to her and she turned away and when she looked back he'd gone. She blinked. I am a little drunk, she thought. That was nothing, that was a stranger's kiss. Stop right there.

It was the party night of a conference in Toronto. After five days of papers, seminars and discussions her brain was tired, but her body had woken up. Smoke hung in the air and fogged around the wads of tobacco leaves that dangled from

161

the ceiling like sad Christmas decorations. This was probably the only public place in Toronto where smoking was not only allowed but encouraged. And he had taken advantage, she had tasted it in his kiss. She didn't smoke, but was capable, it seemed, of smouldering.

She had another drink, got into a conversation about five-year olds, felt a deep pang thinking of her daughter... felt another as she glimpsed the profile of the almost-stranger.

She tore her eyes away and forced her mind back onto the funny little things they say. At the end of the evening, as she was putting on her coat, he came up close behind her. She didn't turn, had no way of knowing it was him except the way all the cells in her body orientated themselves his way, like iron filings swivelling towards a magnet. She felt his warm breath on her skin as he leant in close to her ear. 'Zoo. Noon tomorrow,' he said. She said nothing, buttoned her coat, jammed on her hat, and left.

Back in her hotel room she stared at herself in the mirror. Mascara smudged under one eye, hat-flattened hair. She reeked shockingly of smoke in the bland, air-conditioned room.

There was a message from John on the phone. He missed her; Nicky had won a prize for colouring-in; the cat had fleas again. To rinse away the smell of smoke she stood under the shower, head back, warm water cascading over her face and body. The shower gel smelled like green crushed leaves.

The kiss had happened at about 10pm, she calculated. Because of the time difference it wasn't yet 10pm at home, therefore, as far as John was concerned, it could not actually have happened. She crawled, still damp, between the flat white sheets. Too many glasses of wine, no dinner, only canapés. She felt hungry for something solid and wholesome, like mashed potatoes. The sheets were cool against the planes of her married body and her head swam. She closed her eyes.

A free day. There was a trip to Niagara Falls planned, lunch included, before the flight tonight. A treat for the delegates. As if we are children, she thought, needing sweeties after some ordeal. The phone rang, a colleague telling her that breakfast was being served. She climbed from the tangled mess of sheets and drew back the curtains. It was a brilliant autumn - fall rather - day, the sky high and glassy blue. She looked down at the silent traffic pulsing along the street, looking at her own green wrist veins.

Can anyone see me here, she wondered, naked woman at the hotel window? She lifted both arms, yawned as she stretched. If someone was watching, let them.

She should hurry, pack, leave her luggage in the lobby, have some breakfast, get on the bus, but she wasn't hungry yet and didn't want to see a waterfall or anything or anyone.

She felt a small nag of guilt. Why didn't she ring John last night? She sat on the bed and keyed in their home number, though he'd still be asleep. She left a message: *Well done to Nicky, see you both tomorrow, lots of love, the flea spray's under the sink.*

As soon as she put the phone down it rang, making her start. She stared at it for three rings before she picked it up. Just someone telling her to hurry up, they were about to board the bus. She opened her mouth and discovered a lie waiting on her tongue. 'Not feeling well,' she said, 'tummy and head.' 'The morning after?' her colleague said, and she agreed.

It wasn't quite a lie, she could feel the aftermath of too much wine and there was still a taint of smoke in the air from last night's clothes - almost the taste of it on her lips.

What would she do instead? Be a tourist? She'd buy presents to take home for Nicky and John. Something extra for Nicky for being such a clever girl. She remembered the colouring competition, Nicky at the kitchen table, so carefully crayoning between the lines of the butterflies and bees, milky forehead furrowed, tongue pinched between her teeth.

She finished her packing, dressed and when she was sure the coast would be quite clear, went down to the lobby and ordered a latté and a blueberry muffin.

She kept her eyes down while she breakfasted, flicking through the tourist leaflets. She could visit the Sky Dome, or ride the elevator up the CNN tower. She could take a ferry to Toronto Island, go to a museum or a gallery - or she could go to the zoo. He won't have meant it, or if he did he'd be sure to have regretted the suggestion, or perhaps forgotten. He was most likely on the bus to Niagara right now. She may even have misheard him. Could he have said 'you' and not 'zoo'? It was just a kiss that's all. A silly accidental kiss.

The zoo was almost empty, the air clear and cold. She snuggled into her long lamb-skin coat and hat. There was just one yellow bus outside and children clutching clipboards and pens rushed past her in pairs, but otherwise there was no one about. What a harmless, blameless way to spend the day, an innocent pleasure, a solitary outing to the zoo. So good to be alone after a week of constant chatter and proximity.

She stopped to watch a group of warthogs scuffling in the dirt and wondered, if he, at the Falls, would be wondering if she was here. Her face heated with the thought. What a fool he'd think her. But he would never know. One kiss that's all. One accidental, drunken, kiss.

She shivered as an icy breeze riffled the yellow leaves around her feet. She went into the nearest building and gasped at the rich, rank stench. Two rhinos stood on the far side of a murky green pool. Preposterous creatures, like some crazy inventions, with their dull, carved plates, log-shaped faces and minute prehistoric eyes. Their little tails fitted neatly in a dung smeared groove between the plates and when they walked it was like old men in carpet slippers, a padded buffing on the concrete floor.

She watched them for a few moments, leaning her elbows on the barrier rail. She was about to leave and search out the great apes, when the door swung open.

'There you are,' he said.

'Preposterous,' was all she could think of to reply. She flushed and gestured at the creatures.

'Preposterous rhinoceros,' he said, taking her in. 'You came.'

She watched one of the rhinos butting its head against the wall.

'I wonder what the plural is,' she said. No use denying that she'd come. She turned back to face him and there he was with his stranger's eyes looking down into her own. His eyes were toffee brown, his black hair sprung with grey. She looked at the finely peaked edges of his lips.

'What?' he said.

'Rhinoceroses or rhinoceri?'

'Search me.' He brought his lips down on her own. Her mouth opened with surprise, tasting smoke overlaid with peppermint. Had he sucked a peppermint in preparation?

'Hannah, isn't it?' he said, releasing her.

She laughed. Two kisses and they'd never been introduced. 'And you are Paul?'

'That's me.'

They stared at each other and though it was warm in the rhino stink, her teeth began to chatter.

'You didn't fancy Niagara then?' she said.

His smile started at one corner of his lips and slid along. 'I didn't fancy *Niagara*,' he agreed.

Her treacherous married belly did a flip. She turned away.

'I haven't been to the zoo for ages,' she said, remembering with a pang the last time: with John on Nicky's third birthday. Nicky with her froggy wellies feeding the rabbits in the petting pen, her little fists stuffed with pellets.

'Nor me,' he said. 'I never thought you'd come.'

'I didn't, I mean, I didn't necessarily think you'd be here,' she said. 'I just thought, zoo, nice day, nice idea.'

'Me too,' he said.

They left the rhinos behind, pushing out into the crisp blue air. She pulled her hat further down over her ears. It was icy, leaves skittered towards them like a swarm of mice.

'Shall we see the big cats?' he asked. 'I suppose you're married?'

'The tigers are over there,' she said, noticing the sign. 'Yes, I suppose I am. You?'

She looked up at him. His lashes were thick, and around his eyes a web of laughter lines. He shrugged, charmingly sheepish as he nodded. 'Kids?' he said.

They swapped the names and ages of their children - though not their spouses - as they watched a tiger prowl from one end of its enclosure to the other, and then flow upwards to stand high on a rock, gazing past them as if they were nothing, distance in its eyes.

'Beautiful,' she said, 'Isn't that the most beautiful thing you've ever seen? It's so vivid - so,' she searched for a suitable word, 'so tigerish.'

'Burning bright,' he said, inevitably. 'Can we,' he was looking up at the tiger, 'I don't do this, honestly, but can we go back to the hotel? Get a cab?'

'I came by public transport.' She winced at the prissy sound of her voice. 'Let's see the gorillas first.'

The hairs on her arms prickled towards him, she feared that if she took off her hat, her hair would flow out and wind around his arms. This was not a feeling she had ever had and this was not something she would ever do, something as corny as having a fling with an almost stranger on the last day of a conference, having a fling with the father of Alfie - who was the same age as Nicky almost to the day.

Fling, she thought, it sounds so careless and young. It sounds harmless.

He took her hand. The fine leather of her glove against the wool of his. His big strong fingers clasped her own. A different hand hold, John's was less insistent and their fingers always interlaced, friendly and loose, hands that knew each other. These fingers were tight and strange and sent quivers travelling up her arm.

'Gorillas first,' he agreed, 'and then we jump in a cab.'

He pulled her against him, the buttons of his coat against her face. Taller than John and bigger altogether. She felt sheltered by his bulk.

As they pushed through the doors into the gorilla house, a trail of children came out, excited and shrieking, beating their fists against their chest. About the same age as Nicky - and Alfie. She looked up at Paul, was he thinking the same? But he met her eyes and smiled into them in a way that told her no.

Behind the tall wire fence, the gorilla enclosure had trees and caves, nets to climb, ropes to swing on - a little sample of gorilla heaven.

Paul let go of her hand and removed his glove, then he took her hand in his and eased off her glove. She watched as his long fingers with the little black hairs on the backs and the clean, blunt nails, peeled the leather away from her skin. And then he held her naked hand in his and this time his fingers slid between her own, so snugly, so intimately, it took her breath away.

They were being watched. In the foreground of the enclosure a female gorilla squatted, regarding them with serious eyes. Without looking away she reached out, and with a cushioned palm drew her baby to her breast. The baby opened its mouth, clamped onto her pendulous nipple and closed its eyes.

Gorilla milk, she thought, how much like human? She felt, as she sometimes did watching another woman feeding a baby, a prickle of memory in her own breasts, a twinge of envy and nostalgia.

Nearby, a gigantic silver-back - surely the alpha male - sprawled on the ground, drowsy, scratching delicately between his legs with long gentle nails. A young gorilla clowned with a red bucket, putting it over his head, loping a few yards and taking it off to see where he was. Hannah laughed. She wished Nicky was there to see.

'Seen enough?' Paul said, circling his thumb in the palm of her hand. 'Let's find a cab. We can be back in half an hour.'

The gorilla mother made her lips into a soft tube and grunted as she stroked the back of her child. Hannah met her eyes and flinched at the serious bright brown gaze. Something passed out of her like a breath. She looked down at the pale knot of clasped hands that hung between herself and Paul, at his busily circling thumb.

The mother gorilla flicked Paul a look, got up, child dangling from her breast, and loped away, the knuckles of her free hand scuffing the dust.

Hannah removed her hand from Paul's and put her glove back on.

Linda Lee Welch

was born and raised in the USA. After doing a BA at the University of Alaska, working in radio, and teaching in the Inupiat village of Barrow, she came to England to do a short course at RADA in London. She owned five acres of land north of Fairbanks, Alaska, and planned to travel some and then go home and build a house. But after her course she joined a band and ended up settling down.

Since coming to the UK she has worked as a musician, community artist and teacher. She is currently a Senior Lecturer at Sheffield Hallam University, and also runs Creative Writing groups in the Sheffield Community, as well as poetry and music residencies in schools. Her band, Jackalope Tales, plays regularly around and about.

Linda Lee has won prizes in the Bridport, York, and Jersey poetry competitions. She won a commission to write a piece for the 2001 Off the Shelf Literary Festival, a piece that contained poetry, script, and songs, and was accompanied by her band. Her writing has been published in Ambit, Mslexia, The New Writer, Staple, Young Hippo Spooky Poems, Sheaf, and Sheffield Thursday, among others.

The Leader of the Swans, her first novel, came out in February 2003 on the Virago imprint. The Artist of Eikando, her second novel, also with Virago, came out in November 2004.

In October/November 2002, Welch spent two weeks as a guest lecturer at Meikai University in Chiba, Japan.

She has since been involved in many collaborative projects with musicians, film makers and visual artists, including Flossie Paper Doll (2009), The Woods (2010), Goat Boy and Other Journeys (2011) and Critters (2013).

The Ghost Baby

The woods were deep and dark and Kristin was afraid. Moss squeaked beneath her feet and pine needles stuck sharply into her ankles, making her start with each step. Jays jabbered, all manner of bugs buzzed and droned. The breeze seemed to torture the treetops so that they gasped in response. The ghosts and larger beasts remained out of sight, with only their restless hungry breathing to remind Kristin that, yes, they were out there, and not far away either.

Kristin had been here before, she was sure of it. With breadcrumbs and a brother? Or was it two sisters and a broom? She'd slept here once, for a long long time. But she wasn't sleepy now - quite the opposite. It was daytime for one thing, though in this dense and demented forest she might be forgiven for thinking otherwise. These wily woods kept their hourglass on tilt.

She struggled through a prickly thicket and came out, covered in blood and sweet berry juice, into a pocket handkerchief of a clearing. In front of her were a small table and a chair. The table was set for writing; a magpie quill pen and acorns of ink lay next to a thick pad of paper. Kristin sat down and thought about her situation.

She hadn't wanted to come here. She liked her story. Troubled though it was, it abounded with both woe and wonder. It was her story and not anybody else's, and it was true. But there were others who didn't see it the way she did, and there had been attempts on her life.

The wounded fairy, the tin soldier, the bearded lady, the unkissable frog, sisty uglers and prancing winces all kept mum in the bush. But the ghosts rustled and hissed like snakes: they were multiplying. Kristin picked up the pen and began to write.

2

Two sisters, Bea and Kay, grew up in a gypsy caravan. Their father Jay was a holy-rolling revivalist, and their mother, Dee, made elixirs of uncommon power and effectiveness, recipes passed down from her mother and grandmother. She also read palms for money, which displeased the Preacher Jay somewhat. But folks didn't seem to mind the heathen nature of Dee's fortune telling, and besides, every dollar helped. People always wanted to get a glimpse of the up-and-coming if they could, and Dee very often got it right.

The family were never in one place for long. When a community was rinsed clean, saved in spirit, and cured of afflictions of the body and mind, they'd move on to the next town. The girls were educated by their mother and by life itself. Kay and Bea learned to read from the Bible and the Farmers' Almanac, learned to count by collecting money and keeping accounts, learned to cook and sew out of necessity. They were smart girls, and it showed.

Jay was grooming Kay to join him in the pulpit. At twelve, she could quote the entire Bible by heart, chapter and verse. Jay knew a good thing when he saw one, and would bring Kay on towards the end of his show and get people to shout scripture at her.

'Deuteronomy 6, 4-9!'

'Hear, O Israel…'

'Jeremiah 1, 5-8!'

'Before I formed you in the womb I knew you…'

And so on. Bea's job was to rattle the collection plate harder and harder during Kay's performance, reminding the congregation that Kay's genius needed nourishment. It always worked. But Bea hated it.

Her mother was teaching Bea how to mix and stir and distil the potions. Bea hated that too. From the age of ten, she'd felt increasingly like a mugwump; this wasn't her party anymore, and she wanted out. She began plotting.

3

A sudden high wail emerged from the woods, sharp and piercing and shooting through the air like hard hurricane rain. Kristin jumped up, covering her ears. But the sound went as quickly as it had come: a williwaw, a fluke. Just keep going, she told herself, and sat back down to the job. Just keep going.

4

One Christmas, when Kay was sixteen and Bea had just turned fifteen, they found themselves in a frozen valley town, population thirty-seven. They were kindly invited to set themselves up in a barn out of the cold. Cee Cee Rider, the tough old mare who pulled the wagon, needed a shoe, and a warm place to rest her sore foot.

Kay and Bea picked snug corners on opposite sides of the stables. Kay had been finding pins and needles in her bed, or broken glass, or irritating herbs. She knew it was Bea, but she hadn't said anything yet. She was baffled by her sister's behaviour, and wanted to understand it. But the truth was that Kay spent most of her time in a world apart, a moony meandering place, and earthly things didn't impact so much on her. It was annoying, yes. But minor. Which really got Bea's goat.

That night the heat of the meeting was fierce. These people were desperate for salvation. A blizzard had blown in, and the barn was wrapped round with pummelling wind and blinding snow. When Kay stood to do her thing the folks went mad. The farmer's son, Donald, was entranced, and fainted at her feet. Kay didn't notice, but Bea did. Bea'd had her eye on Donald from the start.

Later that night, when everyone had gone, Donald came back. Dee and Bea had gone to bed. Jay and Kay sat near a fire, staring into it.

'Welcome, Son,' Jay waved him in. 'Sit with us.'

Donald couldn't stop staring at Kay. He sat down on an upturned log and mumbled, 'Kind of you, Preacher Sir.'

They sat in silence for a time. Then Jay stood and stretched his long bony arms over his head. 'I'll be turning in, I guess.'

'Night,' said Donald.

Kay nodded at her father, and he turned and climbed up to the loft where Dee was sleeping. Donald's knee was pumping like a jackhammer. He waited until no more noises came from the loft, and then he pounced.

With one hand over her mouth and one under her skirt, Donald pushed Kay into a pile of hay. It was over in a minute. Kay wasn't sure exactly what had happened. Her mother and father made love in the caravan, but that took some time, by the sound of it. This was more like a first kiss, only there hadn't been any kissing.

She sat up, straightening her skirt and running a hand through her hair. Donald looked perplexed and overheated. 'You sure are pretty,' he said, looking at the ground.

Kay smiled. 'I think I'll go to bed now.' She stood and walked with Donald to the door, where he said goodnight and was gone.

Bea had seen it all. This won't do, she told herself. No Sir.

The next morning rose bitter cold but dazzlingly bright and calm. Dee and Kay made breakfast while Jay chopped some wood for the fire. The hatchet was high in the air when the farmer rushed in. 'My son! He's gone! Look!'

He held out a note which said, 'Gone to the city with Bea. Will write.'

'Bea? Mother, where's Bea?' Jay scanned the barn quickly.

'Gone,' Dee answered. 'I've seen it coming for awhile now.' She handed him a cup of coffee. 'She'll be OK.' She turned to the farmer. 'They're going to be fine. Two kids - boys, I reckon.' She turned to Kay now. 'And then there's this one.'

All eyes were on Kay. 'What?' she said.

'What?' the farmer echoed.

Jay sighed. 'Donald came in here last night and picked on Kay. Did he, you know...?'

Kay shook her head. 'No. I guess so. I'm not sure.'

'Well, I'm sure. You're pregnant,' her mother said.

'Pregnant?' Kay's hands automatically went to her belly.

5

Kristin sighed and put down her pen. This was where it would get sticky, and she knew it. Sticky/tricky/iffy. Swamp and gulf, morass/moraine. Quicksand. 266 babies are born in the world every minute. Why not me? Her story was a kind of baby too.

She held her breath and wrote fast. The wind picked up around her, scattering leaves and leaving pollen in her hair.

6

Jay and Dee and Kay went back on the road when the weather cleared and Cee Cee Rider's foot was better. Things went on as usual. The family had certain towns where they picked up mail and supplies. Six months after the blizzard time they picked up a letter from Bea. She and Donald had gotten married in the city and had a baby on the way. They were deliriously happy and in love with their new life.

Kay had been swelling too, and in late September of that year gave birth to a lovely and robust little girl, Kristin, who, by the time she was five could quote from scripture as well as her mother. When Jay and Dee retired, Kay and her daughter settled down on a smallholding and grew market vegetables and flowers, specializing in rare tulip varieties and scented stocks. Kristin, in her turn, married and bore five children of her own, naming them all after tulips: Elegens Alba, Purissima, Scarlet, Viceroy, and Semper Augustus.

THE BABY

Mystical moonlight, coming on midnight
Hush now baby's sleeping
Sing her a lullaby, weave her a spell
We'll have no woes or weeping
Count on your fingers, wish on a star
On toward the morning we're creeping
One more child in the world tonight
Hush now baby's sleeping.

7

Kristin sat back in her chair and put the pen down. She rubbed her wrist as she scanned the woods. Silence, and then a scraping sound. Something was pawing the dirt. Something growled, and something howled, and Kristin shivered.

She'd been sent to these monstrous woods with only a dry biscuit and a small bottle of dark rum. She reached in to her pocket and pulled out a red bandana, which held her food. She unwrapped the biscuit and shoved the bandana back into her pocket. The biscuit broke apart in her hand, and it was all Kirstin could do to get a few crumbs in to her mouth before it disintegrated completely. A tear pulsed out of the corner of her eye, and then another.

Her fingers ached and her belly was rumbling. If she didn't get it right, she'd never be allowed home, and she might never eat again.

Go back, go back.

8

When Donald came into the barn that night, it was Kay who pounced. And not long after, Bea pounced too. Bea, who loved her sister terribly, and only ever wanted to help, delivered a crunching upper cut and a ballsy knee to the belly. Donald watched amazed as Kay crawled out into the frigid dark, whimpering and defeated. Bea was clearly the woman for him.

Kay suffered a dangerous bleed and had to be left to recuperate with the farmer and his family. She never saw Bea again, though Kay dreamed of her often, and Donald of course, and their wonderful sons.

Kay caught up with her parents seven months later, in high summer and high-bellied bloom. As a fallen woman, she wasn't much use to her father anymore. She birthed a beautiful but sadly stillborn girl and eventually got a job as a telephone operator in a middling town. She waved her mother and father off down the road for good then; they all thought it was for the best.

What stayed with her forever was scripture. It bounced around her brain like Bingo balls and she never knew what number would drop down and show itself until it did. There is no remembrance of former things, nor will there be any remembrance of later things yet to happen among those who come after. Ecclesiastes 1:11.

THE GHOST BABY

Maniac moonlight, coming on midnight
Hush now, baby – stop
Don't wake the goblins the ghoulies and ghosties
You might be in for a shock
Count on your fingers, wish on a star
For deeper in darkness we're creeping
One less child in the world tonight
For you there'll be only weeping.

9

Kristin stood and stretched. She peered warily into the forest, watching for news. A squirrel chittered, but that was all. She picked up her story and sighed. The day was darkening as Kristin hauled herself through the thorny hedge once more, and disappeared.

Marina Lewycka

Marina Lewycka was born of Ukrainian parents in a refugee camp in Kiel, Germany, after World War II, and grew up in Sussex, Doncaster, Gainsborough and Witney. She now lives in Sheffield.

Her first novel, 'A Short History of Tractors in Ukrainian' was published in 2005 when she was 58 years old, and went on to sell a million copies in thirty five languages. It was shortlisted for the 2005 Orange Prize for Fiction, long listed for the Man Booker prize, won the 2005 Saga Award for Wit and the 2005 Bollinger Everyman Wodehouse Prize for Comic Fiction.

Her second novel 'Two Caravans' (2007) (published in US as Strawberry Fields) was short-listed for the George Orwell prize for political writing.

'We Are All Made of Glue' was published in 2009, and 'Various Pets Alive and Dead' is her most recent novel, published in 2012, bringing together hippies, hamsters and the financial crisis. Her short stories have been broadcast on BBC radio, and her articles have appeared in the Guardian, Independent, Sunday Telegraph and Financial Times.

She is now working on her fifth novel. In her spare time she used to enjoy walking and gardening.

The Sad Scotsman

Far, far away in a land by the sea
There lived a sad Scotsman named Mighty MacFee,
He lived in a house at the top of a tree
With a cat called MacTiger, and a dog called MacPee.

MacFee would play reels on his old highland fiddle,
The cat tried to snooze, while the dog did a piddle.
They would stand on the seashore and gaze at the sky
Then they'd sit down together and all start to cry.

The waves billowed in on that faraway shore.
Cried MacFee, 'We are three, but once we were four!'
They sobbed till their eyes were all red-rimmed and raw,
Then MacPee peed discreetly, while MacTiger would roar.

It is true. The sad trio indeed had been four.
Their friend and companion from ages before
Was a bird named MacJoy, who had lived in the tree
With MacTiger, MacPee, and the Mighty MacFee.

The bluebird MacJoy, with her glorious song
Had enchanted her friends all the summer's days long.
MacFee played the fiddle, MacTiger would rest
MacPee, he just piddled - that's what he did best.

The song was so sweet in its musical power
That the fiddler grew jealous, his temper grew sour,
He sulked and he schemed, then one day in a rage
He shut up MacJoy in a small wicker cage.

MacJoy beat her wings on the bars, but in vain.
Her voice grew too weak, and her heart was in pain.
She would surely have died had she not been set free
By MacTiger the cat, or the dog called MacPee.

Now angry MacFee starts to bellow and shout,
'I want to know who let that sodding bird out!
Who has defied me? Who dares to meddle?'
MacTiger just smiled and MacPee did a piddle.

He fumed and he raged and his face turned bright red,
MacPee and MacTiger hid under the bed.
But it was no use, for do what he may
The bluebird MacJoy had flown far, far away.

After some weeks, or a season maybe,
A deep gloom fell over the house in the tree.
With no music except Mighty's squeaky old fiddle
There was nothing to do except grumble and piddle

Summer waned into autumn, and winter loomed near.
The seashore was windy, the tree house was drear.
'Oh, woe!' cried MacTiger, MacPee and MacFee,
'Come back bluebird MacJoy! We're so sad being three!'

Spring came and went, with blossoms in May,
The leaves were all green, but their hearts were still grey.
Cried the Scotsman, 'We just can't continue like this!'
The cat miaowed morosely, the dog...

The sorrowful three hatched a desperate plan.
'We'll go down to the sea, yell as loud as we can,
And maybe the bluebird will answer our plea
And come winging home to our house in the tree.'

Next morning at dawn they went down to the sea,
MacTiger, MacPee and the Scotsman MacFee,
They took a deep breath, and let out such a yell
That it carried their words o'er the waves and the swell.

'Come back bluebird!' they shouted, 'Come back to our tree!
We won't lock you up, you will always be free!
We'll feed you on cherries, and join in your song.
We love you and miss you. We admit we were wrong.'

Those last words, MacFee found the hardest to say,
But he swallowed his pride. He had learnt the hard way
That happiness flies like a bird on the wing.
You can't lock it up and expect it to sing

They sat down on the seashore and gazed at the sky.
The sun rose behind them. The hours went by.
Then on the horizon a small speck appeared
That grew larger and bluer. They jumped up and cheered.

Yes, it was MacJoy, their melodious friend,
Looking happy but tired at her long journey's end.
She wiped a tear from her eye with her wing-er-tips blue,
'I'm so glad to be back. I've missed you all, too.'

Paw in hand, wing in paw, the three who were four
Did a dance in the surf on the edge of the shore.
They sang and they splashed and cavorted in glee,
MacTiger purred loudly, MacPee…

Rony Robinson

Sheffield born of Welsh heritage, Rony is a writer, teacher, broadcaster and father.

He also pretends to be 37.

His most successful work is the novel/radio play/theatre play/opera/musical 'The Beano' (published by Faber), which tells of a northern brewery's works outing to Scarborough just before the Great War, and has been published/performed everywhere.

He wrote 'Last Loves' for Radio 4 with Sally Goldsmith, his own last love, and they won Sony Awards and prizes galore for it.

He has presented Radio Sheffield's morning show for thirty unbroken years, without a mistake, and was in a short list of five this year for the Sony/Radio Academy Award for the nation's best speech broadcaster, alongside Melvyn Bragg and Jane Garvey.

'Ray Hearne', the poet and song writer who features in Rony's story, is Ray Hearne the poet and song writer who ran the famous radio poetry classes on his programme.

Rony's three children, Goronwy, Eleanor and Megan, are all involved in performance and teaching.

Rony plays the Autoharp, has a dog 'Jack', and a cat 'Tempuss', and has never married.

Fahrenheit 4591

1

Dear Bill,

Apologies!

You kindly invited me to submit a piece for your new book. You said you'd like something 'emotional, lyrical, strange, downright poetic', as long as it represents the inner me: 2500 to 5000 words.

So many stories, though! And so little time.

Each venture is a new beginning, a raid on the inarticulate. With shabby equipment always deteriorating in the general mess of imprecision of feeling.

How do we start?

I planned to tell a story that examined storytelling itself, and what it does to teller and told. I wanted to explore how the disadvantaged use story; and discover what happy-ever-after endings mean.

I come to this stuff with some trepidation; feels a bit arty-farty, honestly. But my 'inner me' is increasingly interested in and fumblingly understanding of, for example, how many stories can tell themselves simultaneously, in how many voices (cf Ulysses); and who owns those stories (cf history, written by the winners); and how a reader might 'wrongly' read (cf I.A. Richards); and might 'wrongly' read on (cf the McGuffin); and how non-naturalistic parables might be better able to examine not 'the what' but 'the how' (cf Brecht), and therefore hold out the possibility of change.

I am getting more sympathetic to broken narratives, collage, simultaneous dramaturgy, misleading titles, language for its own sake, alienation, epiphanies, howls -

When you cut into the present the future leaks out.

- repetitions, tricks, calques, coincidences, the out-of-the-ordinary out of the ordinary, echoes and homage, lettrism, the storytellings of both Dylans, Sterne, BS Johnson, Mrs Shufflewick and Dos Passos; writing full of hidden quotes, dialect, childhood rhymes, jokes, mistakes, footnotes, bits of overheard talk - and indeed, the kitchen sink.

Real life seems to be increasingly like that; puzzling, and, in spite of real death, comic. And always with that sense of words and time buggering you about.

'Who's there?'
'Nay answer me. Stand and unfold yourself.'

2

The Story of The Vestibule.

Some time in the late spring term of 19--, the boys in form 3/1 at King Edward VII School in Sheffield, having started with the amoeba last September, have finally reached page 221 of Green's Biology, which has just been distributed, one between two.

We are in for a bit of a surprise.

3

I was reminded of this while attempting to bodge into this piece representing the inner me, the funniest tale ever told, more than once, by Tony Capstick the folk singer, about some girls at Grindleford Station[1].

It's late afternoon in Derbyshire. Two scruffy West Riding lads have been laiking about, but it's now time to catch the train home...

4

Pevsner described as 'quite exceptionally ambitious' the William Flockton, Wesley College building that was taken over in 1905 by King Edward VII School. The Palladian buildings are twenty-five bays wide, with a pedimented centre of seven bays, and eight giant Corinthian columns on a ground floor treated as a pedestal.

The spacious paved entrance area on the first floor is reached by a grand outer staircase and is the very public centre of the school. There is a busy corridor between it and the Hall. There is the headmaster's office with its forbidden door. Gowned teachers criss-cross, frowning. Glass cases shimmer with silver cups and shields won and lost by the heroic dead of Clumber, Wentworth, Arundel, Welbeck and Chatsworth.

There are tombstoned honours boards already full of Edwardians who went over the top to Oxford, and never returned.

And then there are the naughty boys, the smoky boys, and the boys who will never win silverware for their house, or go to Oxford, but who now stand itchy and scruffy in full public

---

1. Capstick told such wonderful stories he never needed to listen to yours. If he had to be interrupted - say we were about to go live in our radio studio, or his trousers were on fire again - the only thing to do was shout out the word 'Sex!' He always pricked up at that.

view, letting the school down and waiting to be punished.

This paved entrance is called The Vestibule, and will be important in what follows.

5

Latin is a dead language
Dead as dead can be
First it killed the Romans
Now it's killing me

6

Vestibule is from the Latin vestibulum, the partially enclosed area between the interior of the house and the street.

King Edward's motto, also from the Latin, is *Fac recte, nil time*, and some boys who want to let the school down make jokes about that.

The Latin school song is *Tempus est ut concinamus/ Quis quis Edwardensium!*

This is the most successful boys' grammar school in England, and if it wants to call its vestibule 'The Vestibule' it will.

7

Epiphany [2]
I was sitting upstairs on the number 8 circular bus going to that same King Edwards, and it will have been, oh, three years later, so in about 19--, with my schoolbag reassuringly on the adjoining seat. I was, just before Hunter's Bar, reading an article in the New Statesman and Nation, when I had an epiphany.

---

2. Epiphanies are moments when you suddenly realise something really important, and (once you have) bleeding obvious.

The journalist was pointing out that we live our lives in many stories.

We are the main character in our own.

Or we should try to be.

But we also have important parts in the stories of others e.g. parents, siblings, friends and lovers. We have minor, maybe unspeaking, parts in the tales of scores of other people we overlap, often without knowing.

And then there are all the stories we aren't in but know from the books we've read, like that bloody Moonfleet from 1/1 to the lives-altering Ragged Trousered Philanthropists Uncle Trevor gave me at 14, from all the comics, e.g. Alf Tupper, and from the stories everybody else tells us we have to read, e.g. Hamlet. There are the stories from the news and from the News of the World, especially those featuring April Ashley the racing car driver who changes sex most Sundays, like we will if we don't keep checking.

Then come the films, especially the French ones, especially The Green Mare's Nest[3] one.

And the unending real stories about real people who get gossiped about by real people for ever. And -

So many stories! Democratically mixing up, like when you dream; or when you're dying.

And starting and restarting, not always in the same place, but all running at the same time.

Including of course the story of me on the No 8 having this epiphany, but still making sure I know where my schoolbag is.

---

3. 1958. 93 mins. Poor subtitles. Very rural France, farmers, soldiers, feathery brassy double beds with people underneath as the springs jangle. A woman micturates in the farmyard. No espadrilles.

8

The Story of The Vestibule (cont).

Green's Biology was adequate on the Amoeba.

We had ruled the margins, put the date, listened, made rough notes, written them up, copied the diagram, rulered off, been caned, passed a one-to-ten test and gone on to fish.

But today —

Margins, dates, rulers, listening, rough notes, writing up, copying, rulering, canes and one-to-ten tests are how we learned in those Goveian days.

We trudged page by page, Durrell to Whitmarsh, Ridout to Nairn, Green to Kennedyseatingprimer[4] with novels like bloody Moonfleet, three pages per homework and the cane if you read ahead, till - if we didn't talk like our parents, or to our parents, or go to Youth Clubs - we could, seven years later, become provincial grammar school teachers ourselves[5].

But today —

9

We don't tell our lives beginnings to ends. Or the same way, every time.

We'd need therapy if we did.

10

Amoebae are single-cell organisms, named after the Greek God Proteus because they can change their shape. They have false feet and can reproduce on their own.

---

4.   B H Kennedy's loathed Revised Shorter Latin Primer. 1888. In some schools Revised Shortbread Eating Primer.

5.   I've just realised that Michael Gove looks like one. Those glasses and the red face. And the suits and how he tries to stride. And isn't clever enough to know how clever he isn't.

This information has never been of any use. Nor has how to clause analyse, sine and cosine, decline, declaim, conjugate, parse or differentiate.

Nor, so far, have Caesar's achievements in Gaul, Bunsen burners, tripods and gauzes, the French word for espadrilles (espadrille) or synecdoches.[6]

11

'Right, 3/1? Enter. When you're quite ready. Sit. Open your Greens. Turn to page 221. No silliness, Mr Robinson. And thank you Mr Cracky Jones[7]. Your task today Chapter 14. You do not need to take notes. You do not need to write anything. You do not need to discuss. You will have no test. You have no need of silliness. Perhaps you'd better open the window for us, Mr Roddis, if you plan to do that all afternoon?'

There are two small diagrams on page 224.

12

I may not be remembering this right.

The diagrams might be on a filmstrip from when I'd become an assistant sex teacher myself, fifteen years later at a London comprehensive. Our weekly sessions there were led by the much unmarried deputy head.

'We do not come to school to enjoy ourselves. There is nothing remotely silly about catching babies or VD, is there Mr Robinson?'

---

6   I would have had some use for the uses of the colon (:) and semi-colon (;) but they were so badly explained at King Edwards that I have never dared use them since, until this piece for Bill, in which the inner me is coming out.

7.   Known by all as 'Cracky Jones', no idea why.

Her progressive syllabus required anonymous handwritten questions from the third year, but we were unable to read them.

My own daughters' sex-

13

Tony pricks up. He and his laiking pal are approaching Grindleford station.

14

- education, forty years on, also involved learning how to catch sexually transmitted diseases, plus how to pass round a perishing Dutch cap without silliness.

My daughters, too, were invited to write anonymous questions, though once again their handwriting was unreadable. Luckily they had learned their sex from Just Seventeen magazine when they were at Primary School, and so have been pretty enthusiastic, though often silly, about it ever since.

15

But, oh poor 3/1 in 19--!

Buzzing, fizzing, trying to keep our hands to ourselves, hairier by the day, red knobbed, pumped up, daren't go on a bumpy bus without a schoolbag, all mouths but mostly trousers, using up our supplies, almost blind, but it was worth it, busting, so needy to go the whole hog and nothing but the hog, but any port in a storm. Hands knees and bumpsy daisy. You coming or what? Yes I said yes I will Yes.

16

Tony and his laiking pal reach Grindleford station.
There are two posh schoolgirls on the platform.
'Yours looks a bit scruffy Angela!'
'Good, Deirdre!'

The train comes in, all steamy.
Hasn't got a corridor.
'Make sure you get off at the stop before the terminus Angela!'

17

Another Epiphany.

The teetotal bar at Peter Cheeseman's old Victoria Theatre, Stoke.

I wanted to write plays from real life, but didn't know how to.

I was told the story of Basil Bernstein.

He said working class people tell their stories twice; once briefly, presumably in case they're interrupted by the foreman or by the machinery, or by their own early deaths; and then a second time, with all the details, often in a meandering present tense with dialogue, but without adjectives or adverbial clauses, in idiosyncratic accents and slangs of their own creation.

Basil Bernstein called theirs the closed code, and didn't seem to like it. Educated middle class people, he said, tell their stories in open code[8], in proper English, so that they can quickly go on to theorise and explain. That's why they go to university.

It was suddenly bleeding obvious not only whose stories we should be telling in their theatres, but in whose words - e.g.

18

THERESA

They were the good old days weren't they? The only way to get a little bit of extra money was, if you want a bit of crumpet you pay for it.

---

8. Shouldn't the open/closed be the other way round?

Well it's the only way you got it. It's right innit? You had about fourpence in your purse to go and you said, 'Alright mate give us a tanner'. No, it's right innit? You had fourpence to get over the next day and the old man come home pissed, if he wanted a bit of crumpet, 4d. There's your dinner.

MERVYN

It's the cream of the East End ain't it?

BOB

Salt of the earth.

MERVYN

Old Arthur'd be flattered if he heard you wouldn't he?

THERESA

We used to sleep in separate rooms. So there's some knocking on the walls and he's shouting, You'll be surprised what I'm knocking this wall with. No, he ain't got nothing there now. Have you seen it? No, I don't like looking at it now. I feel sorry when I see it now 'cos there's nothing there now. I feel sorry for it now 'cos there's nothing there. It's like a little boy's. It's a shame innit when they go little like that. When you think years ago it was big as this stick. Used to make my head bang. That's right innit?

BOB

As big as that stick?

MERVYN

If your Arthur had one as big as that they ought to put him in the bleeding museum.

THERESA

I mean if you can't get across the river you could walk over the bridge over it. Couldn't you Bob? You put yours on the table and show us. And you put yours in Omo Merv, don't half make it come up bright.

MERVYN

As big as that stick? Ought to be in a bleeding museum.

BOB

Tell him you told us he'd got one big as that, and I'll ask him to show us.

THERESA

No he will show you if you ask him. Cos I'm frightened to look at it now.

19

Meanwhile, the second of the two small diagrams in Green page 224.

Our earth is about to unflatten.

Look!

Our *mappa mundi*.

Look!

In sketchy one dimension.

Like… a sycamore seed propeller?

Or… a big pigeon??

Labelled in Latin of course.

With… a bit of a surprise coming up.

20

Dylan Thomas was another grammar school boy who joked about the amoeba's ability to reproduce single-handedly, but was very unsure about girls: without the advantage of Green's diagram, he drew his naked girls with mermaid's tails.

A year after Green, when I was in 4/1, standing in the Vestibule being punched until I confessed *ow* that I thought I was going to be a writer one day did I *ow* - the senior Latin master told me to smarten up *punch* and grow up *punch* and try to be more like the intellectual sober sane classicist Anglican TS Eliot and less *punch* like silly Dylan silly Thomas.

Shows how much he knew about either of them. Or me.

And I know who I'd rather have a drink with, then or now.

Or read. (Or write like.)

21

'That's the bell 3/1. Close your Greens. Hand them in. Without silliness.'

'But sir.'

'Stand. Mr Cracky Jones, we'll have that book back please?'

'Just finish looking at this diagram, sir?'

'And Mr Roddis, leave the window open thank you. It's like The Third Battle of Ypres in that corner.'

'Sorry sir, school dinner sir.'

'If you still have any questions you can write them down anonymously, and hand them to me at the staff room. Otherwise we will resume after the vac with Green Chapter 15, Leaves, Flowers and Cotyledons. Go!'

22

Girls get in empty compartment.
Watercolours of Sidmouth and Durham Cathedral.
Luggage racks. Bench seats. Leather window straps.
'Take the kettle off before it boils Angela!'
'Deirdre!'

23

The bit of a surprise was when Green's Biology, opposite the sketchy diagrams, suddenly said -

The male penis is inserted –

24

I planned in my original notes for this piece, Bill, to discuss how far tragedy is, for all the fancy poetry, an immature and boys' grammar school reactionary form, dealing with fated self absorbed privileged individuals - typically princes who can't make up their minds, and kings who want to marry their mothers.

Many ordinary people (sic) have to be killed before the hero (sic) dies, at the very end, when order is restored, after a bit more brutality, and then off we go again.

Comedy, meanwhile, has good parts for women; the people aren't all posh; worlds turn upside down, and we do the turning; order isn't always restored; falling in love is good; most people will get somebody to fall with; nobody dies; time heals; you can have a laugh.

25

The bit of a surprise, though?

Well, not so much that male penis. That is a bit odd, but we all know what one of those is when it's at home. From the Latin, meaning tail.

Odd again, but not too surprising, is that it's inserted, like a missing word might be inserted in an unseen Latin translation.

Not the *v* word, either, which although of course it isn't in Kennedyseatingprimer, is from the Latin and so is in the reference library, and we've looked it up, so no surprise there, and it means a scabbard.

Nor is it so surprising, because we don't go to school to enjoy ourselves, that Green misses out the thing the scruffy boys of 5G talk about all the time, higher up the sycamore than the scabbard, nearer the penguin's neck.

No, the bit of a surprise is-

26

I txt my windy friend from King Edwards, the travel writer, married man and father of two, Miles Roddis -

I was telling Sally last night about Biology at King Edwards and I tried to quote from Mary Green's book. I remember it saying, 'The male penis is inserted into the vagina up to the vestibule.' I explained to Sally about the Vestibule at school. She didn't believe a word of it. I am not sure now this 'vestibule' isn't something I've imag-

27

I could Google of course?

You can Google anything, even half way through a sentence, and then, well, insert it.

We're all proto post modernists now, with our txts, cutting and pasting and apping and mousing, pinching and @rony37 - ing and changing fonts and generally shaking it all about without even having to leave the house.

So yes, let's go Google!

Starting with - Mary Green's Biology?

28

And 70 years and thirty four seconds later, here she is —

Mary Green's General Science for Schools Biology publ. John Murray 1946, 254 pp, illustrated, spine sunned, some foxing. On Amazon, three copies, used from £14.99

Yes! Or no, actually.

29

Miles has txtd back. This is really unusual.

I fear the architectural appendage is one of your own. Best ask Cracky Jones? He could recite that page by heart. Am-

He could. He did. I could. He would. But he's dead. I think. One of those people you're never quite sure are.

30

Google *him*, then?[9]

Find -nothing. Only the song about Crackity Jones[10](1989)

en crushing automovil
chasing voices
he receives in his head
crack crack crackity jones

Oh and this! Look. From bloody Moonfleet[11] by J Meade Falkner[12] (1898) (1898!!!)

Thou wilt have heard how thirteen years ago a daft body we called Cracky Jones was found in the churchyard dead.

Why daft? Why dead? Why thirteen years ago? Who's thou? Whose story? Why? Who made us take a year to read it sixty years later? Why?

Miles txts on –

-am in a chalet on the far north coast of Norway. We've come to see the northern lights but its been pissing it down ever since we woke up.

What's the story morning glory? Who's we, when they're not at home? Waking up together? And what's all this round-the-houses-grammar-school-speak?

I fear the architectural appendage is one of your own.

---

9. Why don't I just go on line and buy Green, foxed as she might be? Because we don't use international book depositories at our house any more for obvious reasons.

10. Cracky Jones though! The only one who could solve the mystery of the vestibule? After the actual day of the vestibule, he took up Biology really seriously. Spent the rest of his teens trying to get girls into trouble, then went to Durham University on a Biology scholarship.

11. Smuggling, a pub called The Why Not, backgammon, Latin, diamonds, codes and a bloke called Elzevir.

12. Arms dealer, made a fortune in the Great War, suffered writers cramp.

Miles thinks I'm making up the vestibule! Or he pretends he thinks I am.

Do you?

Google it then.[13]

Me? Soz. Too many stories, too little time.

31

Guard calls to Tony and laiking pal, still on the platform.
'Get thi tickets punched there lads?'
'Gee o'er mester!'
Tony and his laiking pal get in and shut the door.
Girls cross-legged opposite sides, opposite ends.
Angela asks Tony his name. He tells her, when he remembers.
'I like skiffle.'
'I bet you do Antony.'

32

What the vestibule did.

where no wax is, the candle shows its hairs
the one-eyed monster rears his ugly head
blood jumps in the sun
yes I said yes I will Yes

spout to the rod
in we go
light breaks where no sun shines
up we go
hold tight
first floor
push comes to shove

---

13. You try, if you've not already

the ceiling cracks
fracks
the crocus pokes
the roman pavement quakes
out we go
Punch.
Stand!
Punch.
Don't slouch!
Punch.
Look at the honours board you dishonour!
Punch.
Look at the silverware flashing in corpore sano!
Punch.
Ut concinamus Edwardensium!
Punch
Behold the man!

whenever polyphemus rears
whenever the fruit of man unwrinkles in the stars bright as a fig
wherever no wax is
behold the man
where tails scabbards sycamore penguins
and whole hogs
spout to the rod
when blood jumps in the sun -
i am nobody

33

Write about what you know about. Everyone says.

Though usually it's better to write about what you only nearly know about; muddle on till the canvas speaks back, and you realise what you meant to say all along.

Another Epiphany.

The sculpture's already in the rock.

34

And on we Google.

Next?

Narrow it down to three Mary Greens.

One runs an underwear site in San Francisco. And two ran schools in England.

Goggigoggi!

The foxed, sun-spined Mary Green ran the last girls' grammar in Sheffield; the other Mary Green ran the first girls' comprehensive in London (at Kidbroke.)

Coincidence or what!

And we're only just starting: it's all coincidences once you google: or live long enough.

Who'd believe a school called Kid-broke?

Or that the Kid-broke Mary was known as Molly, and that her deputy was called Molly too!

Or that Kid-broke school is three streets from the artist's first floor flat that smelt of turpentine in 19--, where, vestibule or not, I did, with help, manage the whole hog for the first time, on a Saturday afternoon at the age of 27^{14}, the year before I myself became an assistant sex teacher.

35

Deirdre says, 'As soon as this train departs for Sheffield it enters the second longest tunnel in England and there are seven minutes of dark thereafter.'

The Guard unfurls his flag.

---

14.   Bernard Shaw was 28.

Suddenly onto the platform, through the gushing steam stagger two
chubby women ramblers.
Angela whispers to Tony what she might do for him in the tunnel.
Tony can't hear in all the gushing.
'He's gone deaf, Deirdre!'
'We know why don't we Angela?'
Angela repeats her offer to Tony. No one has ever offered before.
The chubby ramblers waddle and gasp right up to Tony's carriage.
The guard blows his whistle.
The earth begins to move under Tony –

36

I'd hoped, Bill, I might be able to squeeze in something about Ray Hearne the red troubadour who rhymes with where he comes from, Wath-upon-Dearne, and who, once below a time, ran radio writing classes till all South Yorkshire teemed and ladled poetry. He has a terrific song about Our Elaine.

She is standing at the bus stop down the High Street
A broken shopping trolley at her feet
She is calling to her kids but they're not listening
They're dancing round and round in the Thurnscoe Rain

She is wondering where the 226 has got to
An empty Coal Board wagon soaks her through
As if all the years of giving without taking
Were culminating in the Thurnscoe Rain

Our Elaine, Our Elaine
Nothing lasts forever, Our Elaine

She is sick of feigning pleasure at the bus stop
Sick of bargain queues and cheapo shops
She is sick of penny-pinching on the giro
And who can blame her in the Thurnscoe Rain

Our Elaine, Our Elaine
Nothing lasts forever Our Elaine

Till the anger like a blister bursts inside her
As the winter rants and rages down the Dearne
Tomorrow like a second-hand-shop window
Dissolving in an endless Thurnscoe Rain

Our Elaine, Our Elaine
Nothing lasts forever, Our Elaine

The tune's familiar, sounds Irish, but not quite. Ray Hearne told his radio writing classes to borrow from thieves.

He'd borrowed that saying too. [15]

But while we've stopped, what's the McGuffin[16] here that's keeping you reading? [17]

Once upon a young dream
She wore summers in her hair
Lovers' arms were all that she'd need
Circling the square
Summers in her hair

Now the broken shopping-trolley is still there waiting
The kids are laughing, splashing everything
She turns the corner, calls and they come running
And they walk home hand in hand through the Thurnscoe Rain

Our Elaine, Our Elaine
Nothing lasts forever, Our Elaine

37

Another Epiphany.

---

15. He thinks it's Wilde. You'll be surprised when you Google it.
16. A sort of trick to keep you carrying on to the end.
17. Is it- will the bus turn up?

Red Ladder Theatre, Leeds, in nasty pub after a show.

Augusto Boal. And forum theatre.

In which a story is acted out twice, uninterrupted.

When it is played the third time, members of the audience (the 'Specaudience') stop it by calling 'Freeze!' whenever they think someone's being oppressed.

They then join the scene and try to make it end differently.

The audience call out 'Magic!' whenever what's being made to happen doesn't seem likely.

In this 'simultaneous dramaturgy' there can be many endings; some of them happy, if we work together.

38

So e.g. Elaine is oppressed.

Her kids are mucking about, there's no bus and she's just been soaked by a passing lorry. She's getting old too soon, she's poor, she's unhappy, she's leaving home.

Freeze!

What can we change, without magic?

Improve the 226 route? Thurnscoe could get a better bus service generally? Before that though, maybe we should value Our Elaine a bit more? And ourselves. Don't 'other' her, this girl from Benefits Street. The song doesn't.

Love her for the moment when they hold hands and carry on. And give her proper benefits so the shops can sell her proper food.

Get her off to Northern College.

Take transport back into common ownership.

Do something about the old figures where 7 per cent own 84 per cent of the wealth, or the new figures where 20 families at the top are wealthier than the 12.6 million 20% at the bottom.

39

I think, Bill, this lyrical, strange, downright, poetic mix does represent the inner me, unfolded; you can cut and paste and shuffle me in any order, of course.

It's 4591 words with 11 colons and 29 semi colons, mostly used wrongly on purpose.

40

Miles is in Norway.

Freeze.

When they get out of bed (for the second time today), the rain has stopped.

Cracky Jones returns from the dead. Twice.

Mary Green meets Mary Green, and they chew on, oh, Angela Brazils.

Freeze!

Hamlet forms a theatre company and tours As You Like it with Ophelia, because she wasn't really drowned, like Gertrude claimed[18].

'Who's there?'

'Nay answer me. Stand and unfold yourself.'

TS Eliot[19], Proteus and Basil Bernstein fight in the Captain's tower.

Theresa doesn't become young again, but she stays truthful about sex, which is the McGuffin of all our lives, and just as silly and just as much fun at 73.

Freeze!

---

18. Never trust the storyteller: always ask why they're telling that story; and how; and who's paying.

19. I've hidden a TS Eliot quote. I think it's in the worst written and mardiest paragraph of the 354 that make up this story.

King Edward VII School unfortunately has had to be demolished. It was found to be unsafe. In its place is a people's theatre, called The Vestibule, with a real beer bar, and regular performances of Hamlet 2, The Ragged Trousered Philanthropists, Dylan Thomas & Alf Tupper, with some showings of the Green Mare's Nest and a puppet adaptation of Mary Green's Biology telling It how It wasn't.

And Tony Capstick? He's - alive again.

Magic!

He can give himself a happy ending too. What if the chubby women ramblers don't get in his carriage, as they have done every time he's told the story so far?

It would of course mean Tony'd lose the best story of his life - in return for seven minutes in the second longest rail tunnel in England (1893) with Angela.

Sometimes, (another bleeding Epiphany this) it's as hard to choose our endings as it is to get started.

Ruth Valentine

is a published poet and non-fiction writer; her debut novel, 'The Jeweller's Skin' was published in 2013 by Cybermouse Multimedia Ltd..

Ruth lives in Tottenham, North London.

Her story submitted for this anthology, 'Fire', was triggered by a tragic event in multicultural Green Lanes, near her home.

Ruth's Books:

Novel:
'The Jeweller's Skin', Cybermouse MultiMedia 2013

Poetry:
'On the Saltmarsh', Smokestack Books 2012
'The Announced', Sylph Editions 2009
'The Tide Table', Slow Dancer 1999
'The Lover in Time of War', Scratch 1995
'In Cathar Country', Editions La Serre 1995
'The Identification of Species', Slow Dancer 1991

Non-fiction:
'The Making of Queen Mary, University of London' QMUL 2013
'Asylum, Hospital, Haven: the History of Horton Hospital' Riverside Mental Health Trust 1996

FIRE

A man came into my café and set light to his clothes. It was August, a warm evening; it had been muggy all day but by six you don't feel the discomfort any more. I'd served coffee to two of my regulars, Mehmet who works in the carpet shop next door, and his friend, who might be called Altin, something with A. Mehmet kept me talking about my son, who'd just got his A-level results. What he will do, Mehmet wanted to know. Where he going to Uni?

Kieran, my younger son, has always been clever. I knew why Mehmet was so interested, more than just neighbourly concern, I mean. Kieran was the only one of the children along the street to stay on at school, and Mehmet was thinking about his daughter, Ayse, if she should be staying on and going to Uni. Kieran might become a lawyer or an accountant, some profession where he'd be well paid and appreciated. Then, although I'd never tell my son this, the burden would be off me, a little: Kieran could even send money back home, not a lot but some.

The man was thin and not very tall, with dark straight hair, a bit greasy, and long hands. I noticed his hands because he kept fidgeting. I could see straight away he was unhappy. I don't say that to boast; a child could have told you. He looked down at the floor, and at the wall behind the card-tables, anywhere there was no-one looking back. He was wearing a coat, a shapeless sort of raincoat or light overcoat and, given the weather, that too was strange.

Still, if you stopped for every strange customer. I excused myself to Mehmet and his friend and walked towards the man. I thought he might want a coffee and not have the money; that did happen, and as long as people seemed honest I'd play along, tell them they could pay me another time. Better a recognised lie than charity.

I had to explain to the children about all that. All of them, Jamie and Cassie and now Kieran, helped out in the café after school for a while, when they were eleven or twelve I suppose, before they got to prefer their friends' company. Younger still, they liked the café atmosphere, the people sitting and thinking or playing chess or backgammon, all the banter. I never minded them coming downstairs to watch. Sooner or later one of the customers would call them over and get them talking, school or birthdays or whatever it was. Even so, at that age they didn't understand how I could give free coffees to poor people. It depressed me, that. It must be the schools, or maybe the television, teaching children that generosity is for suckers.

There was that forecourt smell that came in with him. I smelt it but I didn't understand. I started to say something, from across the room, 'A cup of tea, is it?' something like that, and then his coat, the old grey coat with the sleeves too long for his arms, was already on fire. I didn't see him do it. In my mind I keep looking, but although I was walking towards him at that moment, I still can't see what he did with his hands.

The flames were leaping up from his left sleeve, and the left side of his coat. I stood still for too long, watching the flame spread across his chest. He must have thrown the petrol everywhere. It was when it reached his tee-shirt that I woke up. I pulled off two table-cloths and poured the water-jug over them and ran towards him. By now he was screaming. I can still see his mouth, wider open than you'd think possible; his perfect white teeth and his dark tongue.

He veered out of my way. The flames caught the cloth on another table. People were shouting and running to the door. I thought too late of the fire blanket in the kitchen. I threw the wet tablecloths at the man, but before they reached him the flames burst out all over him at once. His face disappeared behind them, and his hair.

If only I'd thought of the fire blanket.

It was very late before we were all home. The firemen had gone. The café was full of water and blackened plastic. I had a dressing along my right arm. No-one else, apart from the man, was injured. Marie had phoned Cassie and she'd come down straight away on the train. We sat upstairs in our sitting-room and tried to have some kind of conversation.

Jamie said, 'It'll be covered by the insurance.'

'It is up to date?' Marie asked. 'You did renew it?'

'What about loss of income?' Cassie said. 'Will they cover for that? I mean till you can re-open?'

The room smelt of smoke and burnt rubber. 'I don't know how we can sleep,' Marie said. 'We'd better try, though, hadn't we?'

'Why here?' Kieran said suddenly. He was sitting on the floor by the window, clicking through the ring-tones on his mobile phone till Jamie told him to stop. 'If he was going to set fire to himself, why couldn't he do it somewhere else? McDonald's, why not McDonald's? They'd never notice. It'd be a public service.'

'Shut it, kid,' Cassie said. Then they all waited for me to say something.

I've always thought why-me questions are for spoiled religious, people who still believe there's a headmaster up there, hauling in truants for six of the best. If I said that, Marie would get upset and say I was getting at her; or that night maybe not, but it would come later. There was a pause.

'Did you know him?' Cassie asked. I shook my head.

'Can you imagine,' Marie said slowly. 'To be so desperate. Poor soul. I wonder. I hope he didn't suffer for too long.'

I saw the flames reaching his black hair. Of course he'd suffered. Marie is the one who says the thing the rest of us are too clever to mention, and then we're all embarrassed and grateful to her.

After a few days Cassie went back to Derby. Her husband Nigel was phoning every night; it didn't sound as if he was coping well.

Marie took just two days off from the hairdresser's, mainly, she said, not to have to answer questions. The boys were working nights, both of them, Kieran doing a few weeks alongside Jamie, security guard on a new building in the City. I was the one with nothing to do all day.

I took to going for long walks in the morning. I'd wash up the breakfast things, though Marie said every morning she could do it, and then set off down to the park. The guys in the all-night greengrocers would be putting out more fruit and veg to make up their stands. I love how their shops look, the piles of chillies and carrots and aubergines, floodlit at night, and even in daylight the colours all but fluorescent.

The men all knew what had happened at the café; well, everyone in the neighbourhood knew, it was on the front page of the freebie paper. The first morning they came out one by one, put down their boxes of mushrooms and apricots and shook my hand. Even the ones with hardly any English said, Sorry, mate, sorry, yes? That was the first time I felt like crying.

After that of course it was nods and smiles, and sometimes a nectarine put into my hand, so I'd eat it on my way past the music-shop and the sauna, to the side gate of the park. The trees at that time of year are big and dusty, the plane-bark starting to peel and leaving bright patches of new skin. I wandered around, never quite sure of directions, and reached the lake with the moorhens, or the playground. One day I sat on the swings all on my own, remembering pushing Cassie up in the air, until a small boy with an ice-lolly stood and glared.

Sometimes I saw the face with the collar of flames.

The days were long. I wrote the letters and phoned the insurance people and talked to the police. I went back to the hospital to have the dressing changed. The nurse said she'd been on duty when they'd brought me in: 'You, and that poor soul,' just the same words Marie had used about him.

She chatted a bit, while I searched for the wording for my question. 'Was he… the other man, by the time he got here..?'

'He died in the night,' she said. 'That's the worst thing. It wasn't even immediate.'

She was taken up for several minutes with the dressing. My arm looked like the underside of a lizard or a tortoise, I decided, discoloured and too soft.

'We found out his name,' she went on. 'At least his first name: the ambulance man knew him from somewhere, the pub I think. Alan.'

Alan. I'd had him down as a refugee, from Afghanistan maybe or North Africa; someone with no connections in this country, chaos at home, and hunted by immigration. A man called Alan wouldn't do such a thing. He might take an overdose, or fix a pipe to his car exhaust, or shoot himself if he got hold of a gun. I kept coming back to it, mainly in the night, since I wasn't sleeping: how would a man called Alan get the idea of setting himself alight?

I didn't tell Marie about all this. She'd think I was being flippant, or else I was morbidly obsessed with the man, and should try to forget him. The truth was that I'd felt guilty not to be thinking of him. A man does such a terrible thing, gears himself up to it, the least you can do is remember him. I was still not recognising how bad he'd felt, only worrying about the method. I thought perhaps it was some delayed reaction and I'd wake up in a week or so and cry the whole day long, thinking about him. That, or get in a rage. I'm not a man who loses his temper; but perhaps this sort of thing made you strange to yourself, out of control? It seemed quite possible; and yet I was still calm, as if half-asleep.

The café stood, blackened and boarded up, the fascia I'd once been so proud of cracked across the middle. I knew people were expecting me to start clearing up, get estimates, send in the insurance claim, talk to the loss adjusters; and then organise a surveyor, decorators, new furniture. Or at least sit down and plan the re-opening, impatient, keeping in touch with the regulars. I met Mehmet in the street, as I strolled back from the park one afternoon. There were children in uniform everywhere; the schools must have started up again.

'Michael, my friend,' he said, and put his arm round my shoulders, walking me past my own café to the kebab joint that belonged to his friend Altin.

He'd been there, I thought. Perhaps he would understand. Though I wasn't sure what needed understanding.

Altin brought me a coke and Mehmet a Turkish coffee.

'My wife,' Mehmet said, 'she say Oh the poor man. Your wife too?'

I nodded.

'Pah,' he said. 'You know what I think? I think, what a bastard. You want to die, god forbid, you kill yourself quiet, no? This man he want to make everyone suffer. If he still alive I kill him for this.' He laughed.

I'd thought about this a lot. 'I guess if you want to die, the last thing you think of is upsetting other people. What would it matter? The one time you really are allowed to be selfish. Nothing more can happen to you, literally, nothing.'

'You are too understanding, my friend.' He looked at me. 'I see you every morning, up the street, packet of fags, buy a paper. You are like an old man. Don't get me wrong, I say you this because you need to know it, yes? This bastard man, this suicide, he attack you. You let yourself feel sad, oh the poor man, you never get over, never.'

Perhaps I don't want to get over it, I thought. Perhaps I'd been doing too much getting over. Kieran was about to go to college, staring at a long booklist over breakfast, going out with Jamie to buy a jacket. In two or three weeks he'd be off, and I'd have missed the hours of talk we might have had.

The man Alan, I thought later, waking as usual at three, and sitting up carefully not to wake Marie: the man Alan was a kind of messenger; but he'd gone before I'd had time to learn the code, and I was left with nonsense on a scrap of paper.

From the restaurant Mehmet steered me along the street, round the people buying watermelon or ironing boards, to the betting shop. The men leaning against the walls or standing close beneath the TV screens nodded as he came in and went on gazing.

'This very important for me,' Mehmet said, and took a thick wad of notes from his back pocket. I watched him in discussion with the cashier, serious, for some minutes. Then his harsh laugh, drowning the manic TV commentators, and he took a number of notes off the pack and counted them out onto the counter.

We stood for a while watching a tall filly with a white blaze stepping delicately across the grass. The name Selkie, and the odds and the jockey's name were flashed at the bottom of the screen. 'Tell me,' I said, 'how is it all racehorses are the same colour? Why not skewbald, for instance?' I remembered a song from the sixties, souped-up folk that I used to listen to when I first came to London, and sang it under my breath, close to Mehmet's ear:

'Now Skewbald was a racehorse
and I wish he was mine.
He never drank water,
he always drank wine.'

'That can't be right,' I said. 'It must be 'I'd always drink wine'.'

The under-nourished men by the TV screens looked dully at us and muttered.

'What did you bet on?' I asked. 'Do you want to stay and see it?' He laughed again. 'No, my friend, this one you will not see. Not even Rupert Murdoch show you this one. We go?'

'Just a minute,' I said. 'I just want to see this one race.' I went to the window and put a fiver on Selkie. I was going to tell him what a selkie is, but then they started, a muddle of patchwork shirts, sleeves billowing as they went, and dark brown horse-skin, and the voices getting shriller: 'It's Desmond Dean, Desmond Dean from Ruana, now Riyadh coming up on the inside, can he do it, Riyadh…' I held my breath and strained to make out Selkie and her pink-and-green jockey; and then it was all over, the horses slowing over a long stretch, a man in a tweed jacket coming forward, the names and odds in the centre of the screen.

'Only a fiver,' I said, and we went outside.

Marie said that evening, 'We'll get that chap, Peter Gordon was it, the one that did Eleanor's up in Hornsey, the designer. Make it look bright and cheerful, so people want to come back again. Not too different, not upmarket as they say, just a bit more modern.'

I'd been thinking all day about money, what it means. I turned to Kieran. 'What do you think, then?'

They all look away, the young people, when you ask them a question. It must be the teachers that embarrass them. Eventually he said, 'I think Mum's right. It's not that it wasn't good before, Dad, it was, only you can't get it back how it was, can you?'

'It's all right,' I said. 'I don't want to.' I was touched that Kieran was so careful with me, touched and a little bit irritated. I watched him at supper, leaning his tall graceful body over the table, eating too fast and talking to Marie about the place he'd be living at college. When I was washing up and he was drying, I asked him, 'Now, tell me, Kieran, I want to know. Why is it you're going to University?'

He juggled the mug in his hand and managed to save it.

'What d'you mean?'

'I mean just what I asked, I'm interested. I'm not criticising. I just want to know.'

He moved on to the cutlery, clattering it back into the kitchen drawer. 'I thought you always wanted me to go. I mean, Jamie, it's not his thing, is it, and Cassie… I thought you wanted me to.' He dried the big knife and put it in the block.

'Is that why you're going? Because I wanted you to?'

'Oh, come on, Dad.' He was relieved; it was that sort of question, and he knew the answer.

'Kieran,' I said, 'I'm trying to work out something. I just want to know if you've got a great urge, a burning desire to do something, go to college, become a lawyer, play in the Premiership...'

He finished the knives and started drying saucepans and putting them back in the cupboard inside each other. The smell of potatoes and the sweet smell of washing-up liquid swirled in the kitchen. He said, 'It's not like that at my age, is it? I mean, I don't know anyone like that. Maybe it comes when you're older.'

Or maybe it doesn't, I thought, and let him go.

Mehmet was standing outside the carpet shop. I was on my way home to meet the man who would tell me what my café ought to look like, but I stopped for a word anyway.

'How did you get on with your flutter the other day?'

'My little flutter, eh? Ah, very nice, very nice. My little flutter make me, what do I say? a big flutter.'

'You put it back on again?'

He dropped his cigarette and heeled it out. 'No, not this time. One day I tell you about it. This is my stock market, the betting shop. My investment, eh? Very good investment.'

His boss called out in Turkish from indoors. 'If it's that good,' I said, 'how come you're here working in someone else's shop, eh? Tell me that.'

You have to be careful asking questions like that, but he slapped my shoulder as if it was the best kind of joke.

'Ah, very good, my friend. Very good. Perhaps I don't want a shop for myself, eh? Perhaps I got other dream.' He yelled something into the shop and closed the door. 'Come, we go visit my stock market.'

This time it was just the horses. We stood and watched, and Mehmet consulted an old man with a newspaper, and we both put money on a horse called Ginger Snap, Mehmet twenty and I ten. I was still cautious. I remembered from way back, the building site, men who got paid in the pub on Friday night and blew the rest at the bookies on Saturday, then starved and cajoled with dull eyes the rest of the week. Ginger Snap came in second; I left with thirty-five quid in my hand.

The designer had left a note when I got back. I tucked it into my wallet; I'd have to call him. Alongside it on the mat was the freebie paper. I took it upstairs for Marie. The front and back pages were an advert for one of the supermarkets, the print colours orangey-red and smudgy green. Inside, under the masthead, the headline read: MAN IN CAFÉ INFERNO IDENTIFIED.

I sat down in the hall, next to the coat-rack.

Police today confirmed that the mystery man who committed suicide in a local café by setting fire to his clothing was Alan Pritchard, 31, from Wood Green.

I skip-read two paragraphs.

Pritchard, a shop assistant, lived alone. His landlord, Joe Nkomi, said the deceased had lived for four months in the room in Westbury Avenue. 'He was a model tenant, no problems,' Mr Nkomi affirmed. Pritchard's half-sister, Annie Winston, said from her home in Port Talbot, 'We were all very shocked when we heard the news. Alan has not been in touch for some time but we all miss him and pray for him.' The body was identified from dental records. The Shannon Café was badly damaged in the incident and is still closed.

I never knew there were so many local papers, nor with so little to write about. 'Mr Hickey, what are your thoughts now that the man who destroyed your café has been identified?' 'How would you say this reflects on the problem of community care in London?' I gave no comment to any of them, though one, a young man with a stammer who turned up at ten at night on my doorstep, I was tempted to bawl out for his disrespect.

The article though had set me back to thinking about the man called Alan, and what had made him do something so extravagant. The electrical goods shop he'd worked in was big and busy. I asked about dusk-to-dawn security lighting, and the woman was brisk and knowledgeable, explaining. I bought a battery-charger, and as I paid tried to make my voice casual.

'Is this the place...?'

She opened the till. 'If you're another one of them that want to know about Alan, yes it is. And no I didn't know him, I've just transferred.' She gave me all my change in one rough handful, and turned away to serve a woman in green.

A week later, after the news, Marie came over and stood beside the settee. 'Michael,' she said, 'I want to tell you something.'

She was worn, deep lines beside her eyes and either side of her mouth, her hair a dull brown with the grey roots showing. I said, 'Jesus, Marie, I'm sorry. I've been so caught up.'

'You've been out of reach,' she said. 'It's been hard for us. So what I thought, now that Kieran's away, I'd go up and stay with Cassie for a week or so.'

I seemed to have forgotten all my family. 'Is Cassie OK?' I asked. 'Are things all right with Nigel?'

Marie looked at me straight. I felt emptied with fear.

'Cassie's OK,' she said. 'I'm the one who's not.'

I grabbed at her wrist. 'Marie, please come and tell me. Sit down with me, please.' She let her arm go limp in my grasp, and by that I knew it was no good pleading with her.

'It's all right, Michael,' she said. 'I'm not going to leave you. It's just that I need a bit of looking after, and you can't do it right now.'

When I came up to bed much later she was sleeping on her side, turned away from the door. I got in carefully, not to pull off the covers, and lay up close to her, my arm across her chest. I was waiting for that moment when in her sleep she'd relax into my arms; but it didn't come, and after a long while I moved over and lay on my back instead.

I stood by Port Talbot station and looked around. Since Paddington the clouds had been building up, and now they were slung low like grey army-blankets over the redbrick terraces and steep streets. I'd had an idea of the place more like a village, a high street and a few narrow side-turnings.

In the paper shop a muscular Asian man with a South Wales accent said he never knew surnames, and not always the first name either. In the butcher's they laughed at me: 'Half Port Talbot's called Pritchard.' I was starting to think the whole of my day was wasted, when a thin-faced bleached-blonde woman in Spar looked me up and down and said with contempt, 'Another one come to gawp at the family, are you? What are you, another journalist, or a, what do they call them, ambulance-chaser?'

She turned away from me to an elderly woman with tins of corned beef in her basket, 'Can you believe it?'

I went into the pub, to get back my self-respect more than anything, and sat with my Guinness in the corner by the cigarette machine. The place was all but empty, a couple holding hands by the empty fireplace, and three men in donkey-jackets laughing with the barman. I wondered if everybody in the town would be as protective as the blonde woman. Close communities: but no, I knew from home, there was always someone who'd rather spill the secret. Then I

221

began to feel like the voyeur the blonde woman thought I was. Perhaps I would be better going home. You should be thinking about your wife and children, a voice inside me was saying. Get the café done and provide for them.

When I looked up the men at the bar had turned towards me, as if they had an agreement. 'You don't look like a Welshman, then,' one of them said.

'I'm London Irish,' I said, 'like the rugby team.'

The youngest of them, fair-haired, with a broad flattened face, looked interested. 'I was living in London myself the last couple of years. Shepherd's Bush. It's all right, London, once you get to know it. What part are you from, then?'

'Haringey,' I said. 'Finsbury Park.' I was going to say what I always said, it was the best place in the world to live, but then I thought of the man Alan, and stopped.

'What brings you down here? Work, is it?' This was the first man, fifty or so and stocky. They all seemed hard, tired; out of work maybe, to be drinking here at eleven o'clock on a weekday. I thought of the scornful woman in the shop, and whether they'd run me out of town. I emptied my glass, and went to the bar beside them.

'How are you doing? Another one?'

And then I told them.

'My god,' the barman said at the end, leaning back against the spirit shelves. 'My god, you never think of that side of it, do you? Well, I didn't, anyway.'

'Nor did that poor bugger,' the stocky man said, and downed a long draught of lager. The blond lad said, 'Well, if it's that bad.. ' and looked warily at me.

I heard a dust-cart outside, the clank as it stopped, then a man's voice calling and the motor starting again. They all looked at the one who hadn't spoken, a thin balding man with a slight stoop. He stared at the floor. 'What do you think, then, Bill?' the barman said.

'What's your name?' he said. I told him.

'And what was the name of this café of yours?'

'It's called the Shannon.'

He put out his cigarette in the glass ashtray. 'I'll tell you what,' he said, to the others more than me. 'I won't ring Annie. I'll ring Carl Winston and see what he thinks, and he can talk to Annie if he reckons she can cope with it. If he says no, it's no. Is that understood?'

His voice sounded too deep for a thin man.

'Of course,' I said. 'I wouldn't want to upset her. She's had enough to deal with.' I watched as Bill took his mobile out of his back pocket and moved over towards the fireplace. Then I couldn't stand it suddenly, and went off to the Gents, down a corridor at the back of the building. I took my time, staring in the mirror, wondering what I was doing there. When I got back to the bar Bill had gone. I looked at his friends.

'Don't worry, Michael,' the barman said. 'He's just gone to get her.'

I was back in time to catch the betting shop. I know nothing about rugby, but I put fifty pounds on Ireland against France, and lost and put another fifty on England to lose the one-day cricket against New Zealand, and when they won I asked what else there was at that hour to bet on, and stayed there losing money as fast as I could until they came round and said they were ready to close.

Susan Elliot Wright

grew up in south-east London, left school at 16 with one O-level and married unwisely at 18. After various incarnations as civil servant, mother, adult education tutor, chef, cleaner and pub cook, she reinvented herself by leaving her unhappy life, taking a degree in English and changing her name from Smith to Elliot (Mr Wright came along later).

While earning a living working in kitchens, she trained as a magazine journalist and freelanced in London for a few years before moving to Sheffield to do an MA in Writing at Sheffield Hallam University, where she wrote her debut novel, 'The Things We Never Said', published in 2013 and now a fiction bestseller.

As a journalist, she has published hundreds of features in women's consumer magazines as well as several non-fiction books on health-related topics. She is now primarily a novelist, although she has written a number of short stories, several of which have won places in competitions or been listed for awards. 'Day Tripper' was originally broadcast on BBC Radio 4 in 2009 as part of the Opening Lines series.

Susan's second novel, 'The Secrets We Left Behind' will be published in May 2014. She frequently writes on the theme of motherhood and also loves writing about extreme weather, and about the sea. She is an Associate Lecturer in creative writing at Sheffield Hallam University and also runs public creative writing courses and workshops.

Day Tripper

Ruth doesn't get out much, but today she makes the effort, hires a taxi, and takes her son to the seaside. Today she would like to get a little colour in her cheeks, for right now, her skin is as pale as a cold, plucked chicken.

She sits on a deckchair in front of the shabby, sky-blue beach hut that she and Graham bought when they were first married. Before beach huts were trendy. Before Joel. She glances along the beach, conscious of her untrendy clothes - she buys these, like everything else, second-hand.

The breeze catches her skirt, wafting it up to reveal pale legs. She has good legs, though their shape is not enhanced by the battered Clarks sandals, sensibly moulded to support the foot. The sort of support you need if you spent your teens tottering in five-inch heels. The sort of support you need once pregnancy and time have pulled the beams from your insteps, leaving you flat footed and cumbersome and prematurely middle-aged.

Ruth is not unattractive. In fact, she was once regarded as something of a looker. But these days, she feels like she is fading away. When she looks in the mirror, which is not often, she sees a face without light, a face that has gone out.

She takes off her sandals and wiggles her toes down into the pebbles, feeling the cool, hard, smoothness around her overheated feet. Joel is absorbed in picking up stones from one side of his body and moving them to the other. Now and then he throws back his head and laughs loudly for no apparent reason, drawing the gaze, it seems, of every other person on the beach.

Ruth notices a short, stocky man walking along the shore, carrying a crash helmet. He sits, glancing over his shoulder and catching her eye. Inexplicably, she is discomfited.

At the water's edge, children play in the surf, their squeals amplified in the thin sea air.

'Stones!' Joel says, in wonder and triumph. The children turn and look, aware for the first time of his presence. They look at his pile of stones. They take in the bottle-end glasses, the large, flabby body and the Bob-the-Builder swimming trunks. They probably don't notice the bulky nappy – that's what it is, let's face it – that will need changing soon if he keeps knocking back the Tango.

The children stop giggling and shrieking. They stand, in that way that children do, sun-hatted heads tilted to the side, arms hanging loosely, eyes in their wide faces screwed up in puzzled contemplation, staring at Joel.

'Stones!' Joel says, pointing in delight to the ever-growing pile at his side. A little girl of about four, wearing a white tee-shirt and shorts, puts her thumb in her mouth. Another, in bright orange, whispers something to a third, who points at Joel and says, 'Why've you got those funny glasses?'

'Katie! Come away!' A shiny, fleshy mother comes flip-flopping along the beach and takes the older girl by the hand.

'Sorry,' she says in Ruth's direction, with an embarrassed smile and a sideways glance at Joel. 'Sorry.'

Ruth smiles benignly.

The remaining two continue to stare. The smallest still has her thumb in her mouth, index finger curled tightly around her nose. 'What's your name?' she says to Joel, without removing the thumb.

Joel laughs loudly. Very, very loudly. The sound of Joel's laugh is probably the single loudest thing on the beach. Louder, even, than the speedboats cutting though the sparkling waves, louder than the seagulls screeching overhead, and louder than the excited barking of a boisterous, water-loving collie.

Joel grins. 'Seaside!' he says.

'My name's Rosie,' she says, earnestly, removing her thumb. 'Can I play with you?'

Ruth glances up and down the beach, expecting to see another anxious mother hurrying towards them. But the parents seem unconcerned, looking over occasionally and smiling in the direction of Joel, who is now making another pile of stones with the help of his new friends.

Should she change him before he gets too involved, she wonders, but decides to let him be for a while. She goes into the hut for her book, soothed by the warm wood smell and reassuring creak of the timbers as she moves around.

Back out in the sunlight, she settles to read. She is careful how she chooses her literature these days, finding her capacity for tragedy all but gone. After a few minutes she sighs, takes a pouch of tobacco and a packet of Rizlas from her battered straw bag, rests them on her book and rolls a cheap cigarette. As she does so, she senses that she is being watched. Glancing up, she thinks she sees the man with the crash helmet looking in her direction, but he turns away quickly.

227

Perhaps she imagined it. She lights the thin roll-up, cursing the stray bits of tobacco that come off on her tongue, and goes back to her book, although she cannot concentrate.

Sometimes, like today, she finds sex scenes difficult to read. Joel was two when Graham left, so it's been fourteen years. She often thinks about sex with her ex-husband. Not because she still desires him, but because sex with him is the only sex she can really remember. It wasn't even that remarkable – except, perhaps, for that one time, the day they found out about Joel. That time, the sex was both rough and tender, an intense mix of 'comforting each other' sex and 'hurting each other' sex. Or maybe, as she has often thought since, it was 'blaming each other' sex.

They say that you forget about sex during periods of enforced celibacy, but Ruth disagrees. She's not obsessed, but sometimes, like now, when she glances along the beach and sees the couples luxuriating in the oily heat, she really could do with the reassuring feel of a hot, hard, urgent body against her own. She snaps the book shut.

Looking down towards the sea, she unexpectedly meets the slightly menacing eyes of the man who is now lying on his stomach, apparently watching her. His face, she notices, is badly scarred. An angry-looking, jagged red groove runs from his cheek to his mouth, giving him a grotesque, one-sided smile.

She feels safe at first, staring from behind her sunglasses, but then becomes unnerved as he seems to be looking straight at her. He is dark, 'swarthy', her mother would have said. Ruth seldom sees her mother these days. Their relationship, never good, has suffered since Joel was born. Many times, they've argued about putting him into a home - or 'residential care' as her mother is careful to call it. Invariably, Ruth refuses to consider it.

The last time, her mother had stalked out, slamming the front door behind her.

'Bang!' Joel had said, beaming at Ruth.

'Clever boy!' Ruth had replied, holding him close so that he wouldn't see her tears. 'What a clever, clever boy.'

Once, very briefly, she'd visited a place. In the day room, waxen-faced children sat silent in their wheelchairs, eyes fixed on the television while support workers chatted in the corner. She'd turned and fled back into the clean, bright air.

The man seems to be staring at her. She closes her eyes and leans back, listening to the sounds of the beach. But she can still feel his glare, sharp and hot. She shivers involuntarily and concentrates on the comforting swish of waves breaking on the shore, drawing the shingle back into the sea. Soon, the chatter of a radio DJ, the children's laughter, and the distant hum of a small plane become muted as she drifts into near-sleep.

At first she ignores the sound of someone crunching towards her. The acoustics of a beach confuse distance. But then her skin prickles, and she opens her eyes an instant before his shadow falls across her face.

'I'm sorry to wake you, but...' he gestures towards Joel. 'Your son?' Ruth nods. 'I think he needs some help.'

Someone has given Joel an ice cream, which has melted, coating his face, arms and stomach. Distressed, he is trying to bat away an army of greedy wasps.

Ruth leaps up, stumbles slightly. The man puts out a hand to steady her. He doesn't seem threatening now she's heard his voice, which is unexpectedly gentle, and she mutters thanks and apologies as he helps to calm Joel and get him cleaned up.

She is surprised by his competence with Joel. Gesturing towards the hut she offers coffee, lighting the Primus to prove that she was about to have some anyway. The man accepts, and offers to help her with Joel who is, not to put too fine a point on it, beginning to stink.

'Don't worry,' he says, cheerfully. 'I'm used to it.'

He explains that he cares for his girlfriend, who was seriously injured in a motorcycle accident.

'Yes,' he says, as Ruth's eyes flicker to his scar. 'She was riding pillion.' He pauses, his face darkens. 'They said she'd improve, but it was four years ago and she's still... well, she's still incontinent for a start, not to mention bad-tempered, barking mad and an absolute bitch to live with.'

Ruth is shocked, and lowers her face as she spoons Nescafé into chipped mugs.

'Don't get me wrong,' he says, clearly noticing her expression. 'I still love her.' A shadow flits across his eyes and he looks away. 'Well, I'll always care for her, anyway. But it's nice to escape. Thank God for respite care! What about...' he nods towards Joel. 'How often do you manage to get shot of him?'

His eyes fix hers, waiting for a reply. His stare is intense, incisive. She gulps her coffee, burns her mouth.

'Don't be offended,' he says, 'There's nothing wrong with admitting it's tough. Surely you take time off occasionally?'

Ruth is flustered, unable to answer. Part of her is horrified at the idea of someone else caring for Joel, another part dreams of just one responsibility-free day. The man offers to wait outside until she's finished changing Joel but suggests that she at least let him do the lifting. She nods, and is grateful.

The job done, and Joel deposited happily on the beach, they go back into the hut. Ruth lifts the water carrier, sloshes water into a bowl on the table and begins soaping her hands.

The floor creaks behind her and she feels his touch lightly on her waist. His hand slides down her arm and his fingers stroke the back of her hand as he gently takes the soap and smoothes it over her skin. His fingers slide over her slippery palm in a gesture unmistakably sexual. Her stomach flips, her back tingles. She doesn't even know this man's name. He is disfigured, ugly. What's more, he has a girlfriend for whom he will 'always care'.

His wet, soapy fingers stroke hers, and she can hear his breath, slightly faster, slightly heavier. Or is that her own? She pulls away and the water splashes onto the table. Again, he fixes her eyes with that stare and Ruth realises how very, very much she would like a fuck.

The moment is broken by a delighted squeal from Joel as he bangs an upturned bucket with his spade. Ruth goes outside to find her tobacco, and manages to steady her hands enough to roll a cigarette.

The man takes the Rizla packet from her and writes down his telephone number. People call him Steve, he says, although his real name is Albert. He doesn't admit that to everyone, and he doesn't know *what* his mother was thinking of. When he leaves he brushes his lips against Ruth's, and says he hopes she'll call.

It's been a nice day, Ruth reflects, as she prepares Joel for the journey home. The afternoon has begun to cool, her face is slightly flushed - from too much sun, perhaps, or from the brush of the salty breeze against her skin.

Ursula Stickland

spent half a lifetime wanting to be a writer, but got sidetracked into working as a teacher, advice worker, hospital clerk, lunchtime supervisor and in an arts centre café. She also worked on a Cornish bulb farm and a community bus. Her greatest achievement so far, apart from having two children, was learning to drive a double-decker.

She now lives in Sheffield with her family and works in a small independent bookshop.

Working in the bookshop brought her closer to the process of writing: she heard visiting authors talk about their inspiration and read proof copies of their work.

She joined a local group, Broomspring Writers' Workshop, and began by writing paragraphs, progressed to whole pages and then to short stories. Currently she is on the MA Writing course at Sheffield Hallam University, which has helped her to develop her work.

Ursula is now halfway through her first novel, 'Dancing with Lions', which is set in the Southern Rhodesia of the early 1960s and narrated by Perseverance, the African houseboy of a newly arrived British family.

Piece of Cake

Benjy stirred. Susie clamped her eyes shut and held herself rigid. She'd become an expert in how to fake sleep. He settled. Surely it was too soon for the day to begin. Later on, most likely much later on, considering what had gone on the night before, she was going with Benjy to look over the flat.

The flat was on the first floor above an Italian restaurant and Martha and John had painted the living room purple, the bathroom crimson, the kitchen brown and, so far, Susie hadn't seen the bedroom. But when Martha and John moved out, they were due to move in. Then they'd have to choose curtains and crockery and candlewick bedspreads like real married people. Susie didn't have time to make curtains and didn't care what they ate off. The idea of candlewick made her despair. And she had an essay to hand in on Tuesday. *Reading: A Psycholinguistic Guessing Game – Discuss.*

So far the topic was a bit of a mystery.

Benjy's PhD was a mystery, too. He didn't talk about it much. He usually had a late breakfast and then made an early start at the pub. He'd start studying after closing time, around three o'clock. He was researching the manufacture of milk out of fish waste. Susie imagined great piles of fish heads, thrown into a vat and boiled into broth, with the eyes bobbing up to the surface. She doubted he was making any progress at all. Was there even a shortage of milk? Perhaps all the cows had joined forces in a union and were working to rule.

Bring back free school milk.

Susie twisted her wedding ring. She'd never wanted to get married, but Benjy had ways of insisting. He'd gone on and on at her until she was worn down. *Martha and John got married and they were happy.* It hadn't done any good saying she wasn't ready, because how could you not be ready after five years. When they'd finally been to make the arrangements, goodness knows what the registrar thought.

Not an appointment at the dentist, you know.

She hadn't come up with a wedding dress and just wore the leaf-pattern one, run up last year on the Singer. There'd been whispers. *What on earth is she wearing?* Her best friend insisted she show willing and order a few carnations. Meryl had also baked her a cake.

Susie went to the post office to buy decorations. She flirted with silver horseshoes, garlands and bells. Toyed with frilly white bands to bind round the edge. Fingered plaster pillars to support higher tiers, if there'd been any.

She picked out a happy couple to preside over the whole concoction. Panicked, put the lot back. She searched the shop for an alternative.

Back home, she beat up lemon juice, sugar and egg white, and unwrapped her purchase. The cake was square, and in one quarter she set toy plastic cows knee deep in the icing. The other three quarters were stocked with hens, sheep and pink-bellied pigs. A woman, left arm forever outstretched, scattered corn for the hens. A man dressed in green overalls directed operations from the centre. Susie stood back to admire the effect.

Would *they* be happy, this farmer and his wife?

*

My Dear Jemima, the farmer had written.

So pleased to make your acquaintance at the Farmers' Ball Saturday last.

Oh God, thought Jemima, checking the signature. The tall one with sticking-out ears who trampled my toes. What on earth could he want?

Hoping you will find it convenient to pay me a visit at the above address on an occasion which may be mutually acceptable.

My herd of Friesians currently stands at fifty strong, and not forgetting Saddlebacks fifteen, Swaledales one hundred, and hens (assorted) twenty-five.

This makes for a good mixed farm, with scope for bed and breakfast business, in the right hands.

You will find me a plain man, not forthcoming with flowery words. Allow me to put it this way. I am certain that, should you take up this offer, you will find it to your advantage.

Yours in haste, time for evening milking,

Jeremy Whitebeam.

Jemima kept this letter at the bottom of her underwear drawer. She felt a silk ribbon unwarranted, as he'd never seen fit to write her another.

*

Weddings took place on Saturdays in the Magistrates Court. When you'd taken your vows right in front of the dock, thought Susie, you couldn't help but feel for all the accused who'd had their sentences passed during the week.

Susie and Benjy had married last September and nothing felt right ever since. At Christmas her own sister sent a card addressed to Mr and Mrs Benjamin Taylor. Who was this Mrs Benjamin Taylor, anyway?

*

'I want a wife,' the farmer said to Jemima. He looked her over, satisfying himself as to her condition and temperament.

'I need someone to stir up the swill, bake some good pies and bring up the children. Preferably strong boys who can shift bales of hay.'

'I'll be your wife,' she said to him. 'Quite pleased to forget I was ever Miss Jemima Blackthorn. I will gladly become Mrs Jeremy Whitebeam. I will sing to your hens, slop swill to your pigs and count up your sheep. I will happily sit by your fire and coddle your eggs, sew patches to elbows and set slippers to warm. I will tend to your churning and roasting and darning.'

'Very well,' said the farmer. 'Quit fussing over those hens and come and view farmhouse. Over here, look. Do come in. Big draughty old place, furniture handed down from generation to generation. Take this bed now, family heirloom. Father died in it, I was born in it. Tradition.'

'Indeed it is a fine piece of furniture,' said Jemima, thinking if she checked the state of the springs, she might appear forward. 'And this house is most accommodating, I'm sure. I am most willing to commit myself to married life under its auspices.'

*

After the reception at the Victoria Wine Bar, Susie had stored the remains of the wedding cake in the cupboard under the eaves. There was probably a good third of it left, its icing pitted by the hooves of the animals. According to Benjy she was too fat, so she wasn't supposed to have any. But most evenings she cut herself a slice to eat in private in the downstairs kitchen, always in the same order, marzipan, icing, cake. If questioned about the mysterious shrinkage, she would say she'd sent pieces to all her relatives who'd declined to attend the wedding.

She saved the plastic farmer and his wife, along with their livestock, in a shoe box.

*

'First off, you get pigs, sheep and hens sorted,' said the farmer. I'll see to cows. Men's work, cattle. Why's it so dark in this barn? Bloody miners on strike again? I hope you've got candles put by at the house. Cows still have to be milked, come hell or high water.'

'Jeremy, I thought...'

'Well don't think. Action, that's what's required. You're a farmer's wife now, honeymoon's over, get cracking. Chicken for supper, that'll do me. That scrawny one, half its feathers pecked off. Wring its neck, get it plucked while it's warm, gut it. Save gizzards for gravy. Roast it, just like Mother. Dig up the spuds. Cut cabbage, brussels and broccoli. Apple pie, custard. Can't abide lumps.'

But Jeremy, she thought of saying, *we didn't have a honeymoon.*

Back at the farmhouse, Jemima broke off a sugar rose from the top tier of her wedding cake, saved at the back of the larder for a happy event. She crunched it up, whole. Scrawny one, she thought. He means Henrietta.

*

The week before the wedding, Benjy's mother had invited them round to tea. Something to show her, apparently. But Susie knew it was wrong the second she saw it, in the bay window of his parents' bedroom. It flaunted its curves, swirling up from bun feet to rickety knees, onwards to gilt drawer handles and rising to the three peaks of its swivelling mirrors. A net curtain protected the modesty of its legs. It was white with gold flourishes and no amount of painting or draping would ever disguise it.

But how to refuse? How to say she wasn't the sort who sat at a dressing table on a pink velvet stool to check her panoramic reflection for blemishes? But the new flat was unfurnished and Benjy's mother knew they had nothing but a Teasmade, a cheese plant and a black-and-white telly between them.

*

Saturday night, after the news, they'd brush their teeth and he'd put on clean pyjamas. They'd lie together in the dip of the mattress and when they'd warmed up she'd unbutton his top, but he'd always see to the knot in the trousers. He'd get up on top and the bed would start to grumble and squeak.

When he really got going she'd imagine being on board ship in a storm, with the creaking of wood and slapping about down below like the churning of bilge water. Just when she thought the heirloom bed couldn't take any more, he'd let out a huge groan and subside. And she'd be left halfway there.

'Jeremy, you know when...?'

'Is there a problem?' he said. 'If anyone knows about this job, it's me. Put more bulls to cows than you've had hot dinners. Equipment's all in fine working order, can't dispute that.'

'It's not that... I just need...'

'Try hypnotherapist, faith-healer, palm-reader for all I care. Been no previous complaints, none whatsoever.'

Who were these previous satisfied customers, she wondered?

'Jeremy?'

But he was already asleep.

Light crept into the bedroom round the edges of the curtains. Six thirty, according to the clock on the Teasmade. Please God, don't let Benjy wake now. Last night he'd emptied a whole bottle of Gordon's. It would take a miracle, not just a cup of tea, to bring him round. When he did surface, he'd expect breakfast as well.

Where's my eggy weggy?

Down in the bloody, blasted, buggery kitchen.

Not that you could say things like that, unless you didn't care about the consequences. You'd boil him the egg, bring it up on a tray.

They were meant to share housework.

Under the thumb, Benjy called it.

When it was his turn to do washing he'd let it pile up, overflow the basket, and cascade to the floor. She'd resorted to recycling her t-shirts. Last time, just when she couldn't stand it any longer, he'd bundled it all up and taken it home to his mother.

Susie tried to think relaxing thoughts, imagined lying on a tropical island beach. A remote tropical island where she'd lay bare her jumbo thighs and huge belly right there on the sand and treat herself to ice cream with chocolate sauce. But her mind was cluttered by unwelcome thoughts. In less than a week they'd be moving. Out of this house for post-graduate students and into a home of their own. Along with that iced cake of a dressing table, the first thing she'd set eyes on every morning for the rest of her life.

Benjy seemed to think that now they were man and wife it was all settled. His brother was married and Judy was already expecting. When Susie thought about babies, all she could see was a line hung with nappies, stretching across the horizon into infinity, blotting out her view of the sky.

He was sweating beside her. She felt stifled by the blankets.

*

'Jeremy, why are those cows penned in with the electric fence? Up in the top field?' said Jemima.

'Questions, questions. Heifers, not cows.'

'It's just they don't seem to have much room. And I was worried...'

'Since when was it your job to worry about stock? Poor animals might hurt their sweet little noses? That is the whole point, my dear. I'm training them, getting them used to the fence. One of them gets a shock, the rest observe and take mental note. Nasty wire makes heifer jump. Heifer keeps off.'

'But isn't it cruel?'

'I didn't hear that, Jemima. Let's just say you have a lot to learn. Take fencing. Vital to the farmer for keeping stock in and vermin out. Twenty-seven gates, three hundred and twelve fence posts, a hundred and thirty-three stakes, twelve miles of barbed wire. All to be maintained and kept upstanding. On top of that, electrics to be checked, every day. Any less than five thousand volts and you're in trouble.'

*

Susie eased herself out from under the covers. Benjy was snoring. She grabbed yesterday's clothes off the floor and didn't waste time with breakfast. She opened the cupboard under the eaves and took out what she needed. Sat at the dressing table for the very last time and coaxed open drawers, extracting clothes for the season, a favourite necklace, one towel. Found her mac and umbrella. Tiptoed to the bathroom for toothbrush and spongebag. Unlocked the desk and slid out bank book, birth certificate, passport.

*

Jemima was in his office. Jeremy's desk was one of those high-backed affairs, with lots of compartments. How could you dust when every iota of space was covered in papers? A large collection of bills was impaled on a spike, but other than that, there was no obvious order. She sat on the wooden chair and twirled herself round a couple of times. When the chair came to rest she reached up to empty the top left pigeonhole.

Electric Fence Reference Manual:

...first used in WW1 to contain prisoners of war... lethal fences still used in Far East to control rodents...

He was outside now, walking the fence, to check no cunning beast had gnawed through the wire and outsmarted him.

...always disconnect the power supply before working on the fence...

You could tell if it was switched on, because you could hear the black box, ticking.

...each pulse of electricity lasts for a very short time, approximately 500 microseconds ...produced at one second intervals...

The black box was in the barn.

...peak of each pulse can rise to 10,000V...

Just across the yard

...effect can be immediate and long lasting ...mammals receiving a shock in a sensitive area...

Jemima put down her duster.

...an unpleasant and memorable experience...

She turned the page.

...healthy person will not suffer any serious or permanent injury in normal conditions...

She went to the back door, opened it and crossed to the barn. Inside it was dark. No one could see her. She took a deep breath.

...however...

*

The bag was bulging, no room for more. Benjy could wake any moment. So goodbye to her childhood storybooks, her record collection, the wedding gift biscuit tin, disguised as a copy of Great Expectations. Goodbye to One-eye, her old teddy bear. Goodbye and good riddance to the dressing table and farewell to the remains of the cake.

She was away along the corridor, down the back stairs, wishing silent goodbyes to the other tenants.

Thank you to Despina for moussaka and hot baked rolls.

To Lorne for gems of Canadian wisdom. *Don't sell yourself short.*

Sneak through the hall. Out the front door. Down the long drive to the cover of the sycamores. Left, then right, go faster, get further before he woke to his headache and her breakout. Any second he'd be rampaging on her tail, taking it out on the accelerator. If she could just get to the main road. But you couldn't stand at the bus stop, wait half an hour for the Sunday service. Must keep moving.

Hitch a lift. She stuck out her thumb. A Minivan passed, slowed, pulled up at the kerb. A girl wound down the window.

'Going to Shipley?' said Susie.

'Yeah, no problem. Jump in.'

No windows in the back. He wouldn't see her. She stowed her bag and the shoe box. Shut the doors, sat down. Took her watch from her pocket. It was three minutes to eight. Two and a half minutes. Two.

She breathed in.

Breathed out.

Breathed in.

The seconds ticked on.